Please, Let Her Be Real . . .

The woman stopped in front of Longarm, who stared up at the beautiful creature before him in wonder.

Heatstroke? he wondered. The desert heat could do that to a man. Strokes caused visions . . .

Or had one of the owlhoots' bullets blown his head off and he was on a gilt-edged cloud floating toward Heaven with one of God's receiving angels?

An angel holding a whiskey bottle in one long-fingered hand, two water glasses in the other hand . . .

The woman continued to smile down at the dusty, wounded lawman—her teeth were as white as porcelain between the richness of her burgundy lips—as she raised the bottle and the glasses and said in deep, throaty, Spanish-accented English: "You saved my life, amigo. For that I owe you a drink."

Her mouth corners stretched to show more of her perfect teeth, and her breasts strained harder against her dress, widening the V even more. "A drink at the very least, huh?"

TABOR EVANS

LONGARM AND THE SONORA SIREN

JOVE BOOKS, NEW YORK

THE BERKLEY PUBLISHING GROUP
Published by the Penguin Group
Penguin Group (USA) LLC
375 Hudson Street, New York, New York 10014

USA • Canada • UK • Ireland • Australia • New Zealand • India • South Africa • China

penguin.com

A Penguin Random House Company

LONGARM AND THE SONORA SIREN

A Jove Book / published by arrangement with the author

For information, address: The Berkley Publishing Group,
a division of Penguin Group (USA) LLC,
375 Hudson Street, New York, New York 10014.

ISBN: 978-0-515-15434-4

PUBLISHING HISTORY
Jove mass-market edition / May 2014

PRINTED IN THE UNITED STATES OF AMERICA

10 9 8 7 6 5 4 3 2 1

Cover illustration by Milo Sinovcic.

Chapter 1

Custis Parker Long, the deputy United States marshal known far and wide by friend and foe as Longarm, stopped his horse, slipped his Frontier Model Colt .44 from its holster positioned for a cross-draw on his left hip, and flipped open the loading gate. He pinched a cartridge from one of the loops on his shell belt and shoved it into the chamber that he usually left empty beneath the hammer, lest he should accidentally shoot his pecker off.

He flicked the loading gate closed.

As he spun the Colt's cylinder and returned the weapon to its holster, he gazed ahead along the two-track cart trail he'd been following for the past three days through rocky, barren godforsaken mountains stretching forever across an endless hot, parched, sun-scorched Mexican desert home to, as far as he had seen, only rocks, salamanders, more rocks, cactus, and rattlesnakes.

And more rattlesnakes. There were plenty of rattlesnakes. In fact, he'd dumped one out of his boot just that morning.

What appeared to be a ghost town lay before him—cream and tan adobe and stone buildings of every shape and size, and gray wooden stock pens lining both sides of the trail. Windblown sand was mounded everywhere.

Tumbleweeds were jammed up taut against the base of every structure that Longarm could see. Windows stared out from the fronts of the hovels, black as empty eye sockets. A wooden shingle screeched to and fro from its rusty chain beneath a brush arbor. At the far end of the village lay a large adobe church that had been burnt by the sun and worn by the wind until it had attained the color of an old penny.

Halfway between Longarm and the church, the circular stone coping of a well slouched beneath a shake-shingled roof. A bucket hanging from a rope slid back and forth beneath the roof in the hot, dry wind, occasionally banging against the stones.

Longarm wrapped his gloved right hand around the stock of his Winchester '73 jutting from the boot strapped to the right side of his McClellan saddle. He spied movement ahead, and froze. But it was only a coyote passing from left to right across the front of the church at the far end of the abandoned village. The scrawny coyote, trotting along with its head down and tongue out, glanced toward Longarm and then loped back off into the desert from which it had come.

At least, the town looked abandoned, Longarm thought, sliding the Winchester from its leather sheath and quietly pumping a cartridge into the chamber. He looked down at the trail he'd been following and saw the tracks of the eight horses that he'd also been following.

The wind had obscured them. In a few hours, it would likely erase them altogether. But they were there now.

And the gang who'd produced them was likely around here, somewhere, too.

The thought had no sooner brushed across the lawman's brain than, glimpsing movement on his right, he threw himself from his saddle, kicking free of his stirrups and hitting the ground on a shoulder and hip as a rifle crashed.

The bullet plumed dust just beyond him.

He rolled frantically as two more rifles crashed, both bullets kicking up more dust behind him. He rolled off a shoulder and gained a knee, extending the Winchester straight out from his right shoulder, aiming more by instinct than conscious effort, and squeezing the trigger.

The man-shaped shadow that had been hunkered atop an adobe on the trail's right side was punched straight back and out of sight behind the adobe's false façade. Another rifle cracked, blowing up dust six inches in front of the lawman. He glimpsed two more shadows above the roofline on the street's right side, and bounded off his heels and into a crouching sprint.

Pop! Boom! Crack-Cracckkkk! Pop! Boom!

The outlaws were opening up on him, filling the air with the sound of angry bees and the thumps of bullets drilling the ground around his hammering boots. Longarm threw himself into a dive, landed on the well's left side, and came up firing between the stone coping and the roof.

"Aye, carumba!" screeched one of the outlaws in Spanish before doing a forward somersault off the roof of an old adobe in which CANTINA was badly faded.

Smoke puffed above a roof to the left of the cantina. Longarm pulled his head down behind the well as the bullet hammered the top of the coping, spraying rock shards. The ricochet sliced across the side of his neck, evoking a wince. Longarm snaked his rifle over the top of the well and sent the third outlaw dancing back out of sight, tossing his rifle into the air and screaming.

Longarm drew his head back down behind the well. Two bullets pounded the far side of the coping, while a third plumed dust in the trail to Longarm's right. The lawman edged a look around the side of the well just as a shadow dropped behind a pile of rotting, steel-gray crates piled at the mouth of an alley between two adobes.

Longarm opened up on the pile of crates, his bullets punching through the rotting wood and throwing slivers in all directions. A man screamed and rose up from behind the crates, tossing his rifle away like a hot skillet and slapping both his hands to his bloody face beneath the brim of his wagon-wheel sombrero. Longarm used the last shell in his Winchester to drill a hole through the dead center of the outlaw's calico-covered chest, punching him straight back out of sight.

Longarm heard the man's thick body hit the ground with a loud thump. Dust wafted.

Longarm hunkered down with his back to the well, looking around wildly for more shooters as he began punching fresh cartridges through his Winchester's loading gate. Something moved up the street. He paused in his work to stare in the direction of the church.

A man stepped out of what appeared to be a hotel on the street's left side, kitty-corner from the church. He was big, broad-shouldered, large-bellied, and bearded. He wore a striped serape and black Sonora hat, the chin thong dangling to his chest. He flexed his gloved hands around the Winchester carbine he was holding on his right shoulder, and grinned as he moved down the steps of the hotel's adobe brick, wooden-railed veranda and out into the street. He was followed by two more men, all staying about fifteen yards apart as they moved out into the street in front of the church.

They stopped and turned toward Longarm, the wind buffeting the brims of their sombreros and the bottoms of their bell-bottomed trousers. The wind lifted a dust devil between Longarm and the three outlaws. The little cyclone spun off to Longarm's left and collapsed against the side of a stock pen.

The outlaws stood with their feet spread, rifles resting on their shoulders. They stared at Longarm with foxy challenge, the big man in the striped serape grinning. Longarm returned the grin and finished punching cartridges through his Winchester's loading gate. Then he pushed back against the well to help him gain his feet, and racked a fresh cartridge into the Winchester's action.

He stepped out in front of the well, facing his challengers. He glanced toward the buildings on each side of him. He'd killed four of the eight Mexican desperadoes he'd been following since they'd robbed a train carrying army payroll in New Mexico—there'd been four more lawmen in his company, but they'd all been killed along the trail by the men they were trailing—so that left one still unaccounted for.

Most likely, that man was just now trying to draw a bead on Longarm from one of the windows or doorless doorways around him. The three before him were likely trying to draw him into a trap.

He didn't see that he had much choice but to face his three adversaries, however.

Edgily, he took another look around, rolling each eye in turn, and then, spying no one aiming a rifle at him from cover, he turned to the three men standing between him and the church, and returned the big man's grin.

The big man's grin disappeared as he hauled his rifle down and leveled it at Longarm, shouting a Spanish epithet and triggering the carbine in his hands. Longarm leveled his own Winchester and, wincing as one of the big man's bullets carved a furrow across the outside of the lawman's left arm, began shooting and pumping the cocking mechanism, spent shell casings whistling and smoking over his right shoulder to bounce off the top of the well.

One of his bullets punched through the big man's gut, sending the outlaw stumbling back toward the church, howling. The other two started shooting and running toward Longarm, crouching over the rifles that smoked and lapped flames as they pumped one cartridge after another into the actions.

Longarm lunged toward the two, firing.

As one of his bullets tore into the side of the man on the left—a stocky Mexican half-breed with long mare's-tail mustaches—knocking the outlaw sideways and triggering an errant shot toward the left side of the street, the other man continued running toward Longarm. The lawman dropped to one knee and steadied his aim as the third man's bullet blew up dust before and around him and another bullet barked shrilly off the well behind him.

Longarm managed to pump two bullets into the third man, but the man kept running in a shambling, crouching gait on past Longarm, toward the other end of the town's main street. The killer kept firing as he ran, and when he'd emptied his rifle, he tossed it away, screaming, blood welling from wounds in his arms and chest. He dropped to his knees and pulled the two pistols from the holsters thonged low on his thighs.

Longarm fired his own last Winchester cartridge at the third man, cursing through gritted teeth when he saw the bullet merely plume dust over the outlaw's left shoulder. He cursed again when the rifle's hammer pinked benignly against the firing pin.

A gun popped from the direction of the church. The bullet evoked a groan from Longarm, who glanced down to see the thin red line of a bullet burn across the inside of his right, brown tweed–clad thigh, alarmingly close to his equipment. The half-breed with the long mustaches just then gained his feet and went running toward the left side of the street, heading back toward the hotel out of which he and the others had come, triggering another round from the pistol in his hand.

Longarm slid his own Colt from its holster, quickly aimed, and fired. Blood appeared on the side of the half-breed's neck. The man's run turned to a shambling, knock-kneed gait that drove him onto a rotted wood veranda and headfirst into an adobe brick wall with a crunching thud.

As he dropped, Longarm dove down in front of the well as the third man triggered his pistols from forty yards away. The third man's bullets screeched over the top of the well and hammered into the coping stones. Longarm peered around the side of the well to see the third man down on both knees and waving his pistols around, as though they weighed twenty pounds apiece. His lips shone between his stretched-back teeth, and his eyes widened when he saw Longarm poking his head out from behind the well.

As the killer got both his pistols under control, Longarm's double-action Colt bucked and roared three times—*Pop! Pop! Pop!*—and the third man's head snapped back as though he'd been lightning-struck. He dropped the pistols to his sides, triggering each into the street and blowing up dust around him. The dust was like a burial shroud wrapping around and over him.

At the same time, both his eyes rolled up in their sockets, as though to inspect the three quarter-sized holes that formed a near-perfect line across his forehead. The puckered holes turned from purple to red as blood began welling in them and dripping, thick as paint, toward the man's eyes.

The killer gave a ragged sigh and sagged backward across the spurred heels of his high-topped boots, the dust of his last two shots still wafting around him. He flopped like a wounded bird and then lay still.

Longarm rose to his knees and pressed his back against the well, instantly flicking the Colt's loading gate open. Looking around for the eighth outlaw—there'd been the tracks of eight horses, dammit, so there had to be an eighth man around here somewhere—he plucked the spent shells from the Colt's wheel and replaced them with fresh from his cartridge belt.

As he flicked the loading gate home and spun the cylinder, footsteps rose on his right. They were hollow, wooden thuds, and at first Longarm wasn't sure where they were coming from, until a woman stepped out of the same hotel from which the outlaws had emerged.

Longarm blinked. He scrubbed dust from his eyelids, wanting to make sure he was really seeing what he *thought* he was seeing . . .

A beautiful, high-busted young woman stood with long, chestnut hair pulled back behind her head to blow beguilingly in the dust-laden wind. She wore a simple black dress, the top of which was so low-cut that it formed a near-perfect V jutting deep into the valley between her large, upthrust breasts, exposing nearly half of each succulent orb.

The woman strode across the hotel's veranda and stopped, staring out over the rail and into the street at Longarm. She smiled and then turned and walked down the porch steps.

Longarm watched her walk toward him, her side-button, butterscotch-colored, calfskin shoes lifting a little puff of dust with each graceful step. Her legs were long and perfectly turned. He could see the form of each as the dress, which came down only to just below her knees, folded caressingly around her as she walked. Her breasts jounced behind the tight, low-cut top of her dress that all but exposed them. A wide, brown, gold-buckled belt held the dress taut against her flat belly, above the intoxicating flare of her full, womanly hips.

The woman stopped in front of Longarm, who stared up at the beautiful creature before him in wonder.

Heatstroke? he wondered. The desert heat could do that to a man. Strokes caused visions . . .

Or had one of the owlhoots' bullets blown his head off

and he was on a gilt-edged cloud floating toward Heaven with one of God's receiving angels?

An angel holding a whiskey bottle in one long-fingered hand, two water glasses in the other hand . . .

The woman continued to smile down at the dusty, wounded lawman—her teeth were as white as porcelain between the richness of her burgundy lips—as she raised the bottle and the glasses and said in deep, throaty, Spanish-accented English: "You saved my life, amigo. For that I owe you a drink."

Her mouth corners stretched to show more of her perfect teeth, and her breasts strained harder against her dress, widening the V even more. "A drink at the very least, huh?"

Chapter 2

"You're the eighth rider?" Longarm asked the Mexican beauty hovering over him. He glanced around at the dead men lying in growing blood pools. Already, buzzards were circling high over the dusty Sonoran ghost town. "There were seven o' them . . . and you?"

"*Sí.*" The woman curled her upper lip angrily as she glanced at the dead men littering the street around her. "Them . . . and me. They took me from my family's hacienda. They—how you say in English? *Kidnapped* me?"

"You were a hostage?"

"If that means they kidnapped me, yes. You are a lawman?"

"Custis P. Long. Deputy U.S. marshal out of Denver." His badge was in his wallet. He didn't usually wear it when he was tracking badmen, as with the sun shining off of it, it made an alluring target.

"That is a long ways away, señor."

Longarm quirked a smile. "My friends call me Longarm."

Again, the Mexican beauty held up the two glasses in one hand, the bottle in her other hand. "A drink, Longarm?"

Just then the breeze cooled and a dark shadow swept the street. Thunder rumbled. Longarm glanced up with one narrowed eye. The sky to the southwest was nearly as dark as night, and the broad mass was quickly sliding over the town on the heels of a growing wind that was lifting more and more dust.

"I'd love a drink," Longarm said. "But we'd best have it inside. First, though, I better stable my horse."

"You are wounded."

"Ah, hell," Longarm said, pushing off the side of the well. "I've cut myself worse shavin'."

"*Mucho macho*," the woman said jeeringly, setting the glasses and the bottle on the side of the well and leaning into Longarm, helping him to his feet. "You sound just like the fools whose hostage I was. Sandoval and the others."

"Marco Sandoval?"

"Sí."

"Wondered who I was followin'," Longarm said, sniffing the girl's hair. It smelled like jasmine. Her body was warm and supple. She fairly radiated a tough, sexy femininity. He could feel the side of one of her breasts mashing against his ribs, and felt a dull pull in his pants. He tried to ignore the natural male attraction. As for Sandoval, he'd heard of the notorious bandit. He looked at the big man in the striped serape. "That him there?"

"*Sí*, that's the pig there."

"Sandoval, eh? Didn't think he rode as far north as that train he held up. Well, no need to worry about him now. I take it the army payroll money's around here somewhere?"

"I don't know what kind of money it is," the woman said. "But the saddlebags they've been carrying are inside."

Longarm nodded, squinting against the chill wind blowing dust at him and the woman. More thunder rumbled, and the black clouds to the southwest were stitched with a blue-white lightning bolt. The wicked flash was followed a second later by a thunderclap so heavy and loud that it shook the ground beneath the lawman's boots.

"You go on inside, miss." Scooping his Winchester out of the dirt, Longarm saw that his coffee-brown flat-brimmed hat, which had fallen off his head in the dustup, had blown up against a stock trough. "I'll tend my horse and take you up on that drink in a minute!" he shouted to be heard over the coming storm.

"Hurry, Longarm, or you'll be soaked to the gills!" the girl yelled as she gathered up the bottle and glasses and began running back to the hotel. Longarm paused as he donned his hat, taking a moment to admire the woman's long, tan legs exposed by the wind blowing her dress up to nearly her waist.

He'd be damned if she didn't appear to be wearing not a single stitch of underwear . . .

The tall, rangy lawmen in a three-piece suit complete with brown frock coat, tweed trousers, string tie, and low-heeled cavalry boots, shook his head and then began tramping back the way he'd come. With each step he winced at the bullet grazes that the wind and blowing grit were finding and causing to burn even worse than before.

By the time he found his horse sheltering in a narrow break between two dilapidated adobes, the sky was spitting rain. Lightning was flashing and thunder was peeling. The break between adobes was too narrow for the horse to turn around in and flee, so Longarm, working around to the front of the beast, was able to grab the spooked horse's reins and lead the army remount back out onto the windy main street.

He rode the brindle bay, which he'd acquired from the quartermaster sergeant at Fort Huachuca, past the well to a small livery barn sitting across the street from the hotel. Fort Huachuca in southern Arizona Territory was where Longarm had been, finishing up a previous assignment, when the order had come in from Chief Marshal Billy Vail, for his seniormost deputy to try to cut off the gang of Mexicans who'd robbed the army payroll and supply train in New Mexico, on their presumed dash for the Mexican border.

Three days out of Huachuca, Longarm had met up with three other deputy U.S. marshals and a grizzled old Pinkerton agent around the little border town of Comita. The lawmen were also on the Mexicans' trail. Vail had forbidden Longarm and the other badge-toters to cross the border into Mexico even if the gang of desperadoes made it across. But when all four of the other lawmen were ruthlessly murdered from bushwhack by the bunch in a roadhouse, while Longarm had been off scouting trail, Longarm had lit out after the gang anyway.

He'd known two of the dead lawmen well. He'd known the other two well enough not to let an invisible line in the Sonora desert dividing countries deter him. After all, it hadn't done anything to deter the kill-crazy desperadoes.

True, Longarm was going against his boss's orders as well as current government policy—border crossings by lawmen from either country were not officially sanctioned by either government and could ignite a nasty conflict—so Longarm was essentially a rogue agent. So be it. Good lawmen were dead, and he wasn't about to turn his back on them as well as on the men who'd killed them merely because of an invisible line in the sand.

He didn't care if it cost him his job. Some things were worth more than his badge. Deep down, his boss Billy Vail would understand.

Longarm was glad, however, that he hadn't known the gang's identity. If he'd known they were the Sandoval bunch, he might have hesitated before riding after them solo. Now they were dead, his friends had been avenged, and a lovely, buxom señorita who wasn't wearing any underwear awaited Longarm with a bottle and two glasses.

The lawman might not be awarded for his travails by his boss or the government he worked for, but an even higher power had bestowed upon him something better.

The livery barn looked well tended, as though it were still being used, and there was plenty of hay and oats. So when Longarm had tended the brindle bay, fed and watered the horse and stabled it near the eight mounts of the gang he'd been following, he headed back out into the street and closed and locked the barn's heavy doors behind him.

Rain was hammering nearly sideways from a low, dark sky, and by the time Longarm had run across the main street and mounted the porch of the hotel, his soaked clothes clung to him like a second skin. He opened the glass-paned, oak door and stepped cautiously inside, holding his Winchester in both hands as he kicked the door closed behind him and looked around.

Rain dribbled from the crown and brim of his hat, and through the rivulets he could see the woman squatting before the open door of a potbelly stove. She was blowing through the open door on fledgling flames, but now she turned toward Longarm. Her brown eyes raked him up and down, and then she said, "I told you you'd get soaked to the gills. You'd better get out of those clothes. I'm building a fire."

She turned her head back to the open door and continued blowing on the crackling flames.

Longarm raked his eyes from the woman to appraise the hotel. It was a shabby little place, but it looked as though it was still in business. None of the windows were broken, and the bar running along the right wall was relatively clean, even polished. There was a small mirror in the back bar, albeit a cracked, warped, tarnished one, and it was framed in several shelves boasting a few bottles, albeit bottles with faded, yellowed labels. But bottles, just the same.

There were six tables arranged to the left of the bar, around the stove. At the rear, a flight of stairs climbed straight up into the darkness of a second story. To the right of the stairs was a curtained doorway.

Outside, the wind and the rain had built to a roar. It almost sounded like a cyclone that Longarm had once narrowly avoided on the Great Plains. The roar drowned out the sound of the stove's crackling flames. The rain pounded the windows until Longarm thought they would break, and he thought the wind would then blow down the adobe brick walls of this obviously ancient long, narrow building.

Unfazed, the woman grabbed a couple of mesquite logs from a wooden box and poked them through the open door, feeding the growing fire. When she'd closed the stove's iron door and latched it, she rose and turned to Longarm. She dropped her chin slightly, spreading those rich, wine-red lips, and then walked slowly over to him, swinging her hips ravishingly, and placed both hands on his arm.

Tugging gently on his arm, she led him over to a table near the stove. "You must get out of those wet clothes, or you'll catch your death of cold."

Chapter 3

"Who runs this place?" Longarm asked as he allowed the woman to lead him to a table near the potbelly stove.

She turned a Windsor chair out toward the stove and then peeled his soaked, dripping frock coat off his left shoulder. "I don't know. He didn't stay around long when he saw us ride into town."

"Cleared out, eh?"

"Sandoval is notorious in Sonora."

"So I've heard."

She hung his coat over a chair near the stove, which was crackling louder now as the fire grew. Still, because of the hammering rain and thunder, Longarm could barely hear it. Lightning flashed, lighting up the front windows.

"Anyone else in town?" he asked the woman as he jerked his shirttails out of his trousers and began unbuttoning the garment.

"Not that I've seen. This is the only place, I think, that hasn't been abandoned."

Longarm shrugged out of his shirt. The woman stood before him with her hand out, waiting to take the shirt from him. Longarm allowed himself another quick look at her—from those full lips to that well-filled, low-cut dress, to her slender waist and flaring hips. When he raised his eyes again to hers, the nubs of her cheeks colored slightly and her eyes sparked beguilingly. She dipped her chin and tucked her bottom lip under her upper teeth, her cheeks dimpling as she tried unsuccessfully to stifle a smile.

Again, he felt the tug in his groin.

"What's your name?" he asked, handing over his shirt.

As she draped it over an arm of the same chair on which she'd hung his coat, she said, "Claudia Cordova."

"From the Cordova Hacienda?" He'd heard of the Cordova family, who ran one of the oldest, largest haciendas in the entire state of Sonora. It was one of the largest, in fact, in all of northern Mexico.

"*Sí, sí*," the girl said. "You sit. I will take off your boots."

She gave him a gentle shove, and he slacked into the chair behind him. She knelt before him, lifted his left foot onto her thigh, and gritted her teeth as she tugged on his boot. The wet leather had shrunk, so Longarm had to help her with a nudge from the toe of his other boot, and then the left boot came off in the girl's hands.

She rocked back on her heels, and her dress was drawn even tauter across her breasts, the V widening dangerously. She laughed and twisted around to set the boot about three feet away from the stove. "The bastards kidnapped me off the hacienda," she said, leaning forward to attack the other boot, sexily flushed with exertion. "I was out on my horse. They found me at a creek . . . I was swimming . . . naked . . . and, *ach!*"

The second boot came off, and she fell back even farther, laughing. "But don't worry, Longarm," she said, setting the second boot down beside the first one, her chest rising and falling sharply. "While they found me naked, I was not ravaged, as I was certain that I would be. There was not another soul around to help me, so I was certain that I would be savaged, humiliated . . . by the whole gang! *One after another!* But, no. Sandoval was many things, but as it turns out, he was not a rapist.

"He said he had his pride, and his pride would not allow him to take a girl against her will. So he simply kidnapped me, took me along with the gang. He said that he was certain that I would fall madly in love with him, and that it would be *I* throwing myself at *him*, instead of the other way around. That pig! Can you believe the gall of such an animal? Obviously, he was mad."

"They harmed you in no way, señorita?"

"They did not harm me. Oh, they roughed me around a little, but not like you'd think. They ordered me around as though I were a simple peon. Like one of my family's servants! They had me cooking and gathering firewood and tending the horses— such humiliations as that. But at least I did not have to endure those curs stripping me down and hammering away between my legs, sticking their tongues in my mouth and raking their evil hands across my bare bosoms!"

She cupped her breasts in her hands and twisted from side to side, glowering angrily up at Longarm.

"At least I did not have to endure that humiliation. Quick, off with your pants!"

Longarm cleared the large frog that had lodged itself in his throat. "What's that?"

"Off with your pants before you catch your death of cold," she said, leaning forward between his knees and clawing at the buckle of his shell belt.

She expertly unbuckled the belt and tossed her head, silently ordering him to slide forward in the chair, and then she pulled the gun rig out from behind him and set it on the chair with his clothes.

"Uh . . . Señorita Cordova," Longarm said, wincing at the bittersweet pain in his groin. "I appreciate the help an' all, but I think we'd better stop right there."

"You must get out of your pants, Marshal Long. You do not want to get sick. Not out here in this godforsaken desert where there are no doctors!"

"Yeah, but . . ."

"Oh, you are shy."

"Well . . ."

Longarm's ears were as hot a cast-iron skillet perched atop a roaring hot stove.

The woman glanced at his crotch, saw the long, sausage-shaped swelling through his skintight trousers. His three-fourths erect dong was angling up and back over his left hip. He ground his fingers into the slivery arms of the old Windsor and tried not to look at her half-revealed bosom. In fact, he was trying to concentrate on the storm, though it wasn't doing much good.

His eyes would not for the life of him allow themselves to leave the succulent female on her knees before him.

Claudia Cordova raised her eyes to his. They were dark, shiny, and large. "Oh, I see." She looked down at her own cleavage, and when she raised her eyes again to his, there were little, gold lights in them.

Again, her cheeks were red. She hiked a shoulder, and her expression became cool, almost stony. "So, you are a man. In fact, you are the man who saved my life, as I am quite certain that when I did not profess my love for that madman, he would have killed me. And soon."

Her fingers were undoing the buttons on his fly. He could feel their warmth against his cock, his scrotum.

When she finished with one button, she started with another. They tickled him, aggravating his condition. "I know that you are not like them, Longarm." Her fingers paused in their work as she raised her eyes to his once more. "Are you?"

"Your fingers keep doin' that little dance they're doin'," Longarm said through a grunt, unable to take his eyes of her deep, dark cleavage, "you're gonna find out."

"No, I don't think so," she said, dimpling her cheeks again as she continued undoing the buttons of his fly.

She worked with excruciating slowness, staring up at Longarm with an amused expression as she undid the last button and then reached up to pull his pants open. She gave a tug and a grunt, and he rose up in the chair with a grunt of his own through gritted teeth, and she gave several more, harder tugs until she had the wet pants down around his ankles.

She was thoroughly flushed, and several stray wisps of her hair were dangling prettily along her cheeks, by the time she had finally pulled the pants over his stocking feet, removing his right, wet sock as she did. She stared down at the long, thick shaft trying to stand up behind his red, summer-weight underwear, the red cotton material drawn so taut around the organ that the uncircumcised head was clearly delineated.

The shaft was now so fully blood engorged that it nodded with each heavy thud of the lawman's heart. His balls bulged beneath it.

"*Aye caramba!*" Señorita Cordova intoned throatily. "You're hung like a Spanish mule!"

Longarm grunted, fumbled with the bottle on the table to his right, and splashed some whiskey into one of the water glasses. He threw back a large swallow and welcomed the gauzy feeling it sent spoking throughout his body after pleasantly burning his throat and belly. It assuaged if only slightly his self-consciousness under the girl's close scrutiny.

She rose and carefully, slowly arranged his pants over the back of another chair positioned near the ticking potbelly stove. The rain had let up slightly, and the thunder wasn't quite as loud as before. Lightning still flashed sporadically in the hotel's windows, the rain dribbling down them silhouetted against the unearthly light.

The light inside the hotel's saloon was murky, dusky, ethereal. It varied between salmon and jade. As Señorita Cordova turned back to Longarm and removed the brown belt from around her waist and then opened her dress to let it fall to her feet, the strange light shone like the pure water at the bottom of a spring-fed creek at sunset, rippling and glinting as it caressed her marble-smooth, almond-dark skin. It cast two semicircles of purple shadow beneath the full, ripe, uptitled breasts.

It glowed umber atop the fully distended nipples.

Staring at Longarm with a bewitching graveness, her dark copper eyes wide and radiant, she reached up to remove the silver clip from her hair. She tossed the clip onto the table beside Longarm, shook her head twice, wildly, and the lawman could have sworn his cock grew instantly twice as hard as before, as he watched the chestnut mass spill and tumble and curl about her neck, shoulders, and breasts.

"Holy shit."

"You like?"

Longarm poured whiskey into the second glass on the table, and then he added more whiskey to his own glass. He held the second glass up to Señorita Cordova, who took it from him as she slowly knelt down between his knees, bending farther and farther forward, her heavy breasts sloping out away from her chest, nipples still fully distended. She threw back half the whiskey, gave him back the glass, and reached forward to begin unbuttoning his longhandle top.

"Now, we have to get you out of these, or . . ."

"I know," Longarm said. "I'll catch my death of cold."

He threw back the last of his whiskey as she unbuttoned his longhandle top and then peeled if off his broad shoulders and pulled it down his arms. He scooted his ass up off his chair enough that she could pull the bottom out from beneath him. She pulled the longhandles out away from his crotch, and his long, thick cock, suddenly unrestrained, bobbed nearly straight up in front of him before angling back over his belly button, throbbing with each insistent beat of his heart.

Claudia Cordova glanced at the impressive organ and

then met his gaze briefly, implacably alluring, before peeling his longhandles down his legs and over his feet. Then her face acquired a devilish little smile and she leaned forward and pressed her lips to the underside of his swollen mushroom head. It was a brief kiss, and when she pulled away and rose with his longhandles in her hands, he felt the heat of her lips lingering on him. It burned so tenderly, so sweetly!

He thought he was going to spurt all over himself right then and there.

She took her own sweet time arranging his longhandles and then hanging them over the back of another chair. She was torturing him, he knew. Making him wait. He could tell she knew exactly what she was doing by the faint, jeering smile lifting her mouth corners.

Fooling with his longhandles, she stood with her profile to him. He ogled her thoroughly from this angle—the lightly jouncing breasts, the long legs, slender arms, a glimpse of chestnut hair showing beneath the supple flesh of her belly. As she turned back to him, strode slowly toward him, he could see that her snatch was wet, the pink folds glistening in the strange, stormy light still filtering through the windows.

Her breasts bounced only slightly. They were firm as rubber, and the jutting nipples pointed slightly to each side. Longarm leaned forward, grabbed her wrists, and pulled her toward him until she was straddling him, and his cock was nudging the wetness of her cunt.

She laughed huskily and pulled away. "First things first, Longarm." Giving him a coy look, she knelt between his thighs, shook her hair back behind one shoulder, wrapped her right hand around his cock, and held it straight up and down. She leaned over it, lowered her mouth to it, closed her lips over the head.

"Christ!" Longarm grunted, squirming around in his chair as her hot, wet mouth slid down the long, thick shaft.

Down, down, down . . . until she made a faint strangling sound.

She slid her mouth back up the length of the shaft, her lips making a popping sound as they came off the purple head. She sucked a deep breath and then went down for more, licking him, sucking him, lowering her mouth until he could feel her throat contracting wildly against the head. Then she'd strangle again and slide her mouth off of him, take another breath, and go down for more.

She did this for about five blissfully excruciating minutes, and then she came off of him, spittle stringing between her rich lips and the wet head of his cock. She kept her face down close to his shaft and pumped him very slowly, gently with her hand, smiling up at him from beneath her eyebrows that were a shade darker than her hair.

Her hand and his cock were liberally coated with her saliva. It snapped and crackled. As she manipulated him, the jutting nipple of her left breast brushed against his scrotum, increasing his sweet misery, until he was sitting straight-backed in his chair, digging his fingers into the splintery arms, tipping his head back, and fairly mewling like a wolf cub from the depths of his sweet torment.

She must have sensed when he was about to come. She stopped pumping him but kept her hand wrapped around the neck of his shaft. His cock throbbed defiantly against her clenched fist.

"Nuh-uhhh," she said teasingly, smiling, placing her thumb over the top of the swollen head, as though to hold his jism back. "Not yet, Longarm. No, no—not yet, *amigo!*"

Chapter 4

Longarm was at the end of his tether.

He looked down at the woman grinning up at him from over his cock clenched in her wet, right hand, her thumb placed over the top of the swollen head, corking him. She was shaking her head.

Her hand was tight, warm, wet . . .

He leaned his head back once more and sent his thoughts hurling out of the eerily lit saloon, out of the warm fist wrapped around his shaft, remembering a horde of Kiowa warriors galloping toward him from over the top of a west Texas desert hill. He tried to remember the Indians' hooting and hollering and his own racing fear as he ground heels into his horse's flanks and ran like hell.

He'd been outnumbered twenty to one, and if he hadn't managed to lose the Kiowa in a deep canyon, his trail would have ended right there. It had been a long night he'd spent in that canyon, hiding out from the Indians he could occasionally hear, looking for him on foot.

He remembered the cold of that long desert night. His thirst. His hunger. The mournful wails of the coyotes. Or were they really coyotes? Possibly, the sounds were the haunting yammers of his Kiowa hunters communicating with one another as they scoured the canyon by starlight for the white-eyes . . .

"Okay," Longarm said now, loosing a ragged breath. "All right . . . I'm . . . I'm good . . . fer now."

"You think so, do you?"

She smiled, sucking her bottom lip, as she released his cock and then climbed onto his lap, straddling his legs, facing him. Her large breasts were in his face. He buried his handlebar mustache in the deep valley between them, as he'd been wanting to do since he'd first seen her holding the glasses and the bottle. She chuckled lustily, shuddering as his mustache and lapping tongue tickled her.

Rising onto her knees, she reached behind her ass for his cock and slid its head up into the warm, wet folds of her pussy. Longarm pulled his face back from her breasts and gritted his teeth as his cock slid up inside her and she lowered herself down onto his lap.

She bounced up and down on her knees, impaling herself over and over again on his cock. As she did, she leaned forward and ran her hands through his hair, grabbing at it, pulling, tugging on his ears, sticking her tongue into each ear and swirling it.

Her hot breath in his ear and along his jaw added to the thundering sensation of sexual delight that radiated through him from her sweet pussy sliding up and down on his cock and her breasts that he was now massaging with his hands, rolling each jutting nipple between a thumb and an index finger.

When he was driven to the precipice of his fulfillment, he reached around and grabbed each of her full buttocks in his hands and held her up at the end of his swollen head, which felt like an exposed nerve.

Outside, the rain began hammering again hard, as hard as it had before. Lightning flashed. Thunder crashed, sounding like a thousand empty rain barrels rolling down a steep, rocky slope.

"What are you doing?" she groaned, trying to continue bouncing up and down. He'd barely heard her above the renewed vigor of the storm.

"Hold on," he wheezed.

She squealed and raked her chin across his forehead, her pussy contracting and expanding against the throbbing head of his cock.

"Hold on," he wheezed again, gripping her sweat-slick ass even tighter.

"Uh-uh," she said, and forced herself down . . . all the way down until the head of his cock felt as though it were residing somewhere up just south of her throat.

She gave another, nasty little chuckle as she wriggled around on him, mashing her cunt down hard on him, her womb gripping him like a vise and oozing hot honey down the insides of his thighs. Then she stuck her tongue in his ear again, and that did it.

"Shit!" he cried, kneading her buttocks as he exploded inside her.

She threw her head back and loosed a love wail to equal any he'd heard echoing from a wildcat's cave. It was joined by more crashing thunder and hammering rain and wicked flashes of near lightning—lightning so close he could smell the sulfur odor of brimstone.

And still he continued to spend his seed up deep within her.

When his spasming as well as hers finally died, the storm seemed to abate, as well. It had been as though Longarm and Señorita Cordova had been in sinc with the heavens.

She kissed his nose and climbed off of him.

"*Christo!*" she intoned. "I'm going to be walking bull-legged for a week!"

She laughed, grabbed her dress, held a hand over her snatch, and said, "I'll be right back!" She ran behind the bar to disappear through the curtained doorway.

Longarm heaved himself to his feet. He gave a chuckle, brushed a fist across his nose, and then walked over and opened the front door. The cool, damp air pushed against him. It felt good, for he was sweating from both the heat of the potbelly stove and his and Miss Cordova's feverish coupling.

He padded barefoot onto the porch. The rain was still coming down from a low sky that wasn't so dark now as light gray. The lightning and the thunder were drifting off to the east. The dead men lay where he'd left them, soaked but cleansed. They appeared little more than strewn trash in the muddy street, surrounded by small puddles into which more rain was splashing.

Longarm sucked a deep drag of the fresh air, tinged with the fragrant smell of the desert. He could tell the town had been mostly abandoned for a long time, as there was no privy or horse stench to corrupt the storm's freshness.

He hadn't heard Claudia come up behind him, so he jerked with a start when she placed a hand on his shoulder. She smiled up at him. She was naked and lovely, still flushed from their coupling. Her hair was a pretty mess hanging down both sides of her face. She held up the porcelain bowl steaming in her hands. A sponge floated atop the warm, sudsy water.

"We got you out of those wet clothes, now we clean you up."

She began running the sponge lightly across the bullet burn on the left side of his neck. He winced at the burn. Amid the fury of his and the woman's recent rutting, he'd stopped noticing the grazes. Now he realized he had several spots of blood on him, though most had dried and were already beginning to crust over.

He'd always been a fast healer, which in his line of work was a definite benefit.

When she'd cleaned the other sundry grazes, she knelt in front of him and went to gentle, soothing work on the graze across the inside of his right thigh—only six inches beneath his balls. Her ministrations soon had his dong at full mast once more, though it hadn't helped, of course, that while she'd cleaned the wound she'd kissed his dangling member and licked it several times, until it started to come alive, like a diamondback sensing a gopher in its hole.

Now she slid the bowl aside, cupped his balls in one hand, and closed her mouth over his cock.

She gave him one of the slowest, sweetest blowjobs he'd ever enjoyed, and he'd enjoyed a few from none other than the master of fellatio herself, Cynthia Larimer, the bewitching young niece of Denver's founding father and

Longarm's sometime companion. As for this afternoon, there was something about the heat that had built up in him from before by the fire, and the cool, damp air blowing against him now. That and the warm-mud sensation of Claudia Cordova's silky soft lips and tongue sliding slowly back and forth along his cock while she very gently caressed his balls with her hands.

She paused every once in a while to run her tongue from the base of his cock to its tip before slowly—oh, so devilishly slowly—closing her mouth over him once more, and sucking.

When he came, she dutifully swallowed every drop and cleaned him with her tongue. Then she took the bowl and the sponge, gave him a warm, intimate smile and a peck on the chin, and disappeared inside again.

Longarm was chilly now, as the sun was falling, taking the temperature with it. He went back inside and closed the door and began thinking about official business, since it was Sandoval's bunch that had brought him here. For all practical purposes, as long as he was in Mexico against the wishes of his own as well as the Mexican government, he was a rogue agent. If the Mexicans caught him down here, they could shoot him, and the shooter would likely get a commendation.

Even when he got back across the border, he wouldn't be in the clear. Not if anyone from either side knew he'd been down here. But so far, he hadn't been seen by anyone except the men he'd killed and the woman he'd fucked. He doubted Claudia Cordova would tell on him. Longarm saw no reason to tell anyone, either. Including his boss, Chief Marshal Billy Vail.

His getting the stolen army payroll money back would likely be all anyone would really care about. When he wrote up his official report, he'd leave out any and all references to a border crossing. As far anyone would know, he and the other lawmen had caught up to Sandoval somewhere just north of Mexico.

He just had to get back north without being seen by anyone who would care.

The loot . . .

He'd been so mesmerized by Claudia Cordova that he hadn't thought about it until now. He'd noticed gear around two pushed-together tables on the other side of the stove, where the outlaws had obviously been playing poker before they'd been taken to the dance, so to speak. He tramped naked over there now, his bare feet slapping the worn wooden puncheons.

There were three sets of saddlebags—two on a table with three rifles and a pistol and, improbably, a set of dentures and a worn pair of boots. Another set of saddlebags hung over the back of a chair positioned close to one of the chairs surrounding the two tables that had been shoved together to form one long gaming table. Eight chairs surrounded the two tables, each with a nice pile of money on the table in front of it.

In fact, the table was covered with U.S. scrip and specie. Several thousand dollars' worth. Apparently, the thieves had already divvied up the money and had been gambling with it when Longarm had ridden in to spoil their fun.

Longarm opened the front flap of the saddlebags draped over the chair. Several bundles of greenbacks and a burlap pouch of coins resided within. He gathered up the money from the table and shoved it into the saddlebags. He looked around the tables to make sure he'd gotten all of it. There was no point in counting it. He didn't know exactly how much they'd taken off the train, but he doubted the killers had had time to spend much more than a few dollars here and there on their run to the border.

The bags were good and heavy. He probably had most of it.

He set the saddlebags over the back of a chair near the one he'd been sitting in when Claudia Cordova so distracted him. It was growing dusky inside the hotel. He lit a bracket lamp hanging from a ceiling support post, shoved a few more chunks of wood into the stove against the growing, damp chill, and checked his clothes.

His longhandles and socks were nearly dry, so he slipped them on. He also donned his hat, as he never felt quite complete without the old, bullet-torn Stetson riding his prow at a jaunty angle. He'd confiscated several of the outlaws' cigars, as they wouldn't be needing them anytime soon. Yawning, the fatigue of the long ride, the shootout and killing, and the more than pleasant fucking having oozed into his bones, he slacked into his chair and fired a lucifer to life on a thumbnail.

Drawing the peppery Mexican tobacco smoke deep into his lungs, he poured out more whiskey and threw back half a shot. He could hear pans rattling around behind the curtained doorway. A heavy stove door squawked. Soon, a pleasant smell emanated from the same direction, and he sat enjoying the smell of roasted meat and frijoles while he slowly smoked the cigar and sipped the whiskey, which was not his preferred Maryland rye but would do.

He'd no sooner finished the cigar and the whiskey than Claudia came through the curtained doorway carrying a big wooden tray on which several large platters steamed, filling the room with an even keener smell of seasoned meat, gravy, and beans.

"I hope you're hungry, amigo!" she intoned as she moved out from behind the bar.

She'd donned her dress but wore it in a more careless fashion, one breast nearly completely exposed. Her hair was a thick, beautiful mess. She was barefoot. Her bare feet slapped the floor as she strode purposefully over to Longarm's table and set the platter in the middle of it.

"My god!" Longarm exclaimed, standing and doffing his hat in appreciation of both the woman and the meal she'd whipped together.

"This is what I was working on when you came in and culled the herd!" Claudia threw her messy hair back and chuckled through her teeth.

She set in front of the gaping lawman a platter of steak covered in green chili and fried onions and red peppers, with a generous helping of seasoned pinto beans threatening to swamp it. She set another platter no less generously proportioned in front of her own chair, and set another platter of fresh corn tortillas on the table between them.

The steam wafted, thick and aromatic, in the buttery light emanating from the lantern.

"One more thing!"

Claudia wheeled, hair and skirt swirling, and tramped back behind the bar. She leaned down briefly, and when she straightened, she held up a straw-cloaked demijohn, smiling jubilantly.

"Wine," she intoned heartily, grabbing a couple of clean glasses off a back-bar shelf. "Now, my dear lover, we can salute what I am sure will be a long and prosperous union!"

Chapter 5

"*Salute!*" Claudia said, holding up her wineglass.

"*Salute!*" Longarm said, clinking his glass against hers and then frowning at her over the top of his. "Uhh . . . what are we saluting, now . . . Señorita Claudia?"

She sipped from her own glass, licked her lips, and then smiled at him sexily. "To our union, of course. Our *partnership*." She glanced at the saddlebags hanging over the chair between them. "We have all kinds of money, no? Two people—you and me, Longarm—could go very far on such a haul, to be sure."

Longarm set his glass down, frowning. "Well, I reckon we could at that, Claudia. But I think I told you I'm a lawman. A deputy United States marshal, to be exact. It's my sworn duty to follow the law. That's why I'm down here, collecting the money those miscreants laying out there in the bloody mud stole from an army train."

Longarm's scowl deepened. Never once in his long and storied career had he ever considered going wayward.

Oh, with women, of course. There was no official harm in fornication.

But he'd never once considered doing anything illegal. In fact, he'd always made a conscious effort to keep the line between right and wrong very clearly defined before him, and he'd always followed it to a T. True, if you went purely by the letter of the law, he'd illegally crossed the border into Mexico, and he was here illegally now. But he saw that as a small price to pay for a much greater good. He'd be making amends for that well-intended breach soon.

After all, the thieves and killers were dead, his lawmen friends had been avenged, and he'd recouped the stolen money.

He wasn't about to let a woman—even a young Mexican beauty as sexy and erotic as Miss Claudia Cordova—lead him astray into true-blue outlawry.

"Longarm, you are a long way from home," Claudia said over her smoking plate, holding her wineglass in both hands beneath her chin. "As far as anyone from your country would know, you were killed down here, the money lost."

Longarm was incredulous. "And what about you, Claudia? Are you willing to go outlaw in your own country? And why in hell would you even need to? You're from one of the wealthiest families in all of northern Mexico!"

She curled her lip and glanced owlishly down at her plate. "My father is a *pendejo.* A real pain in the ass. He keeps me on a very short leash."

Claudia's eyes sparked with beseeching when she looked across the table at Longarm again. "He has promised me to the son of a friend of his—a young man from a rich family outside of Mexico City. I have met this young man only once, and he is a pimply-faced little whiner. A bony, pale, high-strung, spoiled rich man who never had to work a day in his life. He has no *seasoning*. He is not a man."

She lifted her mouth corners. "He is not a quarter of the man you are, Longarm. I want a man who can make me howl like a she-cat when he makes love to me. I want a man who can make me feel like a *woman*. I want a man like you, Longarm."

She eased her shoulders back slightly, subtly shoving her breasts forward against the wide V of her dress, until her nipples were clearly defined. "I want *you*, Longarm."

Holy Christ, he thought. Staring at her, listening to her words, he'd actually spent all of five seconds considering her proposition. He couldn't believe he'd done that, but he had. For a moment, he'd imagined them together, traveling in style around Mexico City and Europe and, of course, fucking like dogs in the best digs money could buy.

Stolen money.

He swept the thoughts from his mind, got ahold of himself.

"Claudia, I don't think you really mean what you're saying. You haven't thought it through. You couldn't enjoy spending that money any more than I could."

"Ah, *Christo!*" she intoned suddenly, turning her head to one side, her cheeks flushing angrily. "Of course I couldn't!" When she turned back to him, she was smiling radiantly, chiseled cheeks dimpling. She gave a slow blink and again raised her wineglass. "But it was a nice fantasy, was it not?"

Longarm had to admit that it was, as he touched his glass to hers and took a sip of the sweet red wine.

"Now, let's eat before the food gets cold!" Claudia now wished only to regale him in the present.

The lawman needed no further encouragement. He dug in with fork and knife, cutting into the steak and filling a fresh corn tortilla with meat and beans and green chili and fried peppers. His belly groaned hungrily as he filled his mouth with the first bite of the hot, deliciously succulent, and perfectly spiced and flavored meal. He didn't normally drink wine, but its fruity sweetness was a nice complement to the heat of the meal, which seared his tongue and had his ears burning after just the first bite.

But he continued shoveling it in and washing it down with the wine, so hungry that he looked up only a couple of times to see Claudia doing the same thing he was. Longarm grinned at the way she attacked her plate. Not so very different from the way she'd attacked his cock. The big lawman preferred a woman who displayed a hearty appetite rather than one who picked snootily at a plate of food, like it was something to endure rather than enjoy.

Of course, he didn't like them too fat, either. He was absently amused at the irony of his typically male preferences. And they said women were irrational. Hah!

He finished only a minute before she did, sitting back in his chair and giving a hearty belch.

"There's more," Claudia said, standing and reaching for his plate.

He grabbed her hand and shook his head. "If I ate another bite, I'd founder." He pressed his lips to her hand.

"I want to thank you for that wonderful meal, Miss Claudia Cordova. Whoever you do end up marrying is gonna be one lucky man, and I sure as hell hope he appreciates you."

"Ha!" Claudia said as she sat back down in her chair and continued forking the remains of her meal into her beautiful mouth. "Señor Adriano Lorca, whom I've been promised to, eats like a rabbit. He's afraid of getting fat because of course he never does any work to help keep him trim. He only visits tailors and drinks and smokes prissy-looking cigarillos. He attends bullfights, gambles away his father's fortune, and rides his father's blooded horses around a grassy compound at their hacienda."

The ravishing Mexican beauty tossed her fork onto her empty plate, sat back in her chair, belched nearly as heartily as Longarm had, brushed her sleeve across her mouth, and yelled, "*Mierda!* I am doomed, Longarm."

"I got a feelin' you'll make out all right, Señorita Cordova."

Longarm poked a fresh cigar into his mouth and fired a match on the cartridge belt coiled around his holstered Colt, within an easy grab on the table if he should need it. He never knew when he'd need his guns—often he needed them when he'd least expected to—so he always kept them, including the .44-caliber over-and-under derringer he normally wore in a pocket of his vest, as close as possible.

Claudia leaned far forward, so that he could see nearly all of her splendid breasts slanting down inside the dress. "Where do you head now, big man?"

"Back north with the loot. I'll drop it off with the U.S. marshal in Prescott, and head back to Denver and, likely, another assignment that'll take me God knows where."

Longarm touched the match to his cigar and gave her a wink through the wafting smoke. "*After* I've seen you safely home, of course. I couldn't let a woman who looks like you travel alone"—his brown eyes flashed behind the veil of cigar smoke—"even the wildcat that you are!"

She reached across the table to grab his hand. "Before we say *vaya con Dios*, I am going to show you what kind of a wildcat you'll be missing, big man. Upstairs! Just as soon as I freshen up—I have water heating on the stove—and can dig up a bottle of good mescal. Every barman in Mexico has a bottle somewhere of good mescal!"

She rose, grabbed their plates off the table, and hustled back through the curtained doorway but not before Longarm felt his longhandles tighten at the crotch, having admired the sashaying of the girl's firm, round ass behind the tight dress, and her thick hair tumbling sexily across her shoulders.

The wine had grown on him. He poured more from the demijohn and then wrapped his pistol and shell belt around the outside of his longhandles. He was sure he looked ridiculous in the longhandles, hat, shell belt, and socks, but he wasn't about to take in an opera show with Cynthia Larimer on the Denver street named after her family, so he didn't give a rat's ass.

He doubted that Claudia would, either.

He tramped out onto the front porch, instinctively stepped to one side of the glass-paned door that he pulled closed behind him, so he wouldn't be backlit, making himself an enticing target. The Sandoval Gang was dead, but who knew who else was lurking out here? Doubtful anyone would be, after the downpour, but he'd been a lawman long enough to have become a creature of cautious habits.

Cigar cupped in his left palm, wineglass in his right hand, Longarm drew a deep breath of the fresh, rain-scrubbed air. He stepped over to the railing and looked up and down the street. The storm had moved on, leaving some high, thin, gauzy clouds in its wake. The sunset was a faint salmon wash behind black velvet peaks in the west, causing the rain-filled dimples in the street to glow faintly with the same color.

Just as he was about to marvel at the serene silence of the remote Sonoran ghost town, he heard a faint growling off to his left. The growling grew louder, until he recognized the competitive snarls of a couple of wolves and saw the inky skirmish up the street to the west, beyond the well.

Two wolves were fighting over something. Likely one of the dead men. Suddenly there was a high-pitched yip, and that seemed to end the skirmish. Hooves padded wetly in the muddy street, and Longarm canted his head and frowned to get a better view of the four-legged creature trotting toward him. As the beast approached the hotel from the middle of the street, heading east, its eyes glowed above some long object protruding from both sides of its jaws.

Longarm stared at the jostling beast, and then made a face. The wolf had torn an arm off the corpse. A ring on the pale hand extending from the right end of the arm winked in the last light. The wolf's eyes glowed proudly over the trophy in its jaws. The beast did not give Longarm so much as a passing glance as it continued trotting on down the street, splashing through intermittent puddles, its head and the arm held high, before letting the darkness of the eastern mountains erase it from the lawman's view as it headed off to dine in private.

"A better man would have buried those poor killers." Longarm chuckled and took a deep draw off the cigar. He followed it up with a swallow of the wine.

He stood there for a long, relaxing time, one hip perched on the porch rail, smoking and drinking and watching the stars twinkle to life behind the thin screen of clouds. He felt good, and his hunger for food and sex was sated.

At least, he thought it was sated. But then he heard Claudia's bare feet slap in the hotel beyond the door, and she stepped out, the starlight twinkling in her eyes and on the bottle she held in her hands.

"Found the mescal," she said.

She came out, popped the cork, and handed him the bottle. Longarm took a pull and smacked his lips. It tasted like the desert smelled. Heady stuff, as was the girl standing before him.

He gave her back the bottle. She corked it, gave a coquettish little pirouette, placed a hand on the crotch of his longhandles, and waltzed over to the hotel's open door. "There will be more waiting for you upstairs, Marshal Long." She gave him a luscious smile and tramped through the doorway. He stood listening to her bare feet pad across the saloon floor and then climb the stairs.

As trail-weary as he was, he felt the old trouser snake

come to life. He remembered her lips, breasts, hips, the fullness of her supple ass in his hands.

Longarm chuckled. He took the last drag off his cigar and flipped it into the street, where it sizzled in a puddle. Then he went inside, closed the door, grabbed his rifle off the table, grabbed the saddlebags with stolen army loot off the chair, and headed upstairs to find Claudia waiting for him naked, sitting on the edge of a bed, leaning back on her elbows. Her dark body was bathed in flickering lamplight.

She had her heels hooked over the top edge of the bed, knees spread. Her messy hair framed her face, shadowing it. Her eyes glinted in the shadows between those thick chestnut tresses.

Longarm's cock came instantly to attention. He tossed the saddlebags onto a chair. He shucked off his gunbelt, hat, longhandles, and socks in less than ten seconds, and followed his cock to the girl's gaping pussy. He started to lean toward her. She grabbed his jutting hard-on with one hand, and with the other hand she lifted the bottle that had been resting at her side.

"Not that you need it, but it's an aphrodisiac. Trust me. I'm so horny I could fuck all night!"

Longarm took the bottle and threw back two large, delicious swallows. Then he gave her back the bottle, and as the mescal instantly kindled a hot fire in his loins, he shoved her back on the bed. She began mewling, and clawing his back, arms, and shoulders, as he started hammering away between her knees, sucking her lips and lapping her tits.

The vague realization that something was wrong came early in the night.

The realization grew, but he was in such a fog of carnal bliss that he didn't realize the error of his ways until he woke up the next morning, head pounding, to find himself tied spread-eagled and naked as a jaybird on the bed, his lover and the saddlebags filled with stolen army money nowhere in sight.

Chapter 6

"Claudia!" Longarm bellowed, gritting his teeth as he jerked at the ropes tying his wrists and ankles to the bed.

His enraged screams made his aching head only ache worse, but the rage and frustration was too much for him. *"Claudia, come back here, you fucking bitch!"*

After about fifteen minutes of this, lying there helplessly and yelling, he heard what sounded like a footfall on a stair step. Then another. The rickety stairs squawked beneath the weight of someone climbing them.

Longarm lifted his head from the pillow that smelled like his captor's sweet oozings, and said, less shrilly, "Claudia, is that you? If you've come back and you untie me, I won't hold it against you. We all make mistakes. I know how much you don't want to have to go home and marry that pimply-faced kid. I can understand. Just come on up here and untie me, and neither one of us will ever mention it again."

He stared at the room's wide-open door. As he did, he

heard another footfall. This one was much closer. A head slid into view from the side of the doorway. The round, dark, bearded face staring in at Longarm was in such ghastly contrast to the beautiful face of Claudia Cordova that Longarm's heart leaped up into his throat.

"You ain't Claudia," he said, instantly realizing how dunderheaded the remark must have sounded.

The man's black eyes scrutinized Longarm closely, sizing up the situation. And then he moved his whole body into the open doorway—a short, stocky Mexican in a greasy buckskin shirt and soiled duck trousers held up beneath his paunch by a dirty rope. He wore rope-soled sandals, and a bandanna high on his forehead held back a wooly mass of salt-and-pepper hair. He wore a knife on one hip and an old Colt's revolver on the other hip.

Slowly, he moved into the room, his head turned slightly to one side, a dubious look on his round, dark, bearded, pockmarked face.

"Who're you?" Longarm said.

The man did not answer. There was a strange animal quality about him. Longarm got the impression that if he spoke at all, he did not speak English. His nostrils worked, sniffing the air like a deer.

Longarm looked at the gun and the knife, both well used. He was nervous. Tensely staring at the man walking slowly toward him as though toward a leg-caught mountain lion, Longarm said, "I am a deputy United States marshal. Name's Long. Now, if you'll just cut these ropes . . ."

The strange, little, potbellied man stopped beside the bed, sort of crouching as though prepared to wheel and run or to pounce—Longarm wasn't sure. The strange man lowered a thick, callused hand to the bone handle of the bowie knife on his left hip, and slid the knife from its sheath. Holding the knife point-up and turning it slowly, menacingly between his brown fingers, he glanced at Longarm's crotch.

Longarm's balls ached. His dick retracted, like a snake wanting to retreat into its hole.

"Easy, there, amigo," Longarm said, staring up at the man staring darkly down at him. "You just cut me loose, and I'll buy ya a drink. How'd that be? Like I said, I'm a deputy U.S. marshal . . . down here on federal business."

Under the precarious circumstances, he didn't mind confessing that information to this man. What harm could it do? He was already in a bucket of burning oil.

The strange, dark man crouched down close to Longarm's face. His breath smelled like something had died under his tongue. He slid the point of the knife up close to Longarm's throat and said in only slightly accented English, "You're hung like a Mexican mule, amigo!"

With that, his face crumpled with wild laughter. He raised the bowie knife above Longarm's head to saw through the rope tying the lawman's left wrist to the headboard. Still laughing and blowing that awful-smelling breath, he reached across Longarm to cut the rope on his other wrist.

"I had you goin' there for a minute, didn't I?" he said between guffaws.

"You did have me goin', at that," Longarm said, sitting up and tossing away the cut rope from both wrists while the stranger went down and cut the ropes on both ankles. "All funnin' aside, I do appreciate the help."

He sat up, and rubbing the blood back into his hands,

he regarded the man who was still chuckling at his own joke, which he seemed to think was the funniest thing he'd ever heard or come up with. "So . . . uh . . . you live around here, Señor, uh. . . ."

"Estaban Frederico Luis-Jiminez Albion," the man said, shoving the big bowie back down into its sheath. "But you can call me Loco. All my friends do." He nodded at Longarm's naked crotch. "And since I've seen a hell of a lot more of you than I've seen of most of my friends, I reckon we're close enough to go by our nicknames, eh? You got one?"

"Got one what?" Longarm was still on the bed, sitting up. He rested his elbows on his knees and pressed fingertips to his aching temples, gently massaging.

"A nickname."

"Oh. Yeah. Longarm."

"Longarm, huh? Oh, I get it. Longarm!"

Loco tipped his head back and loosed several more loco guffaws at the ceiling. Longarm's temples throbbed as the man's voice careened against them, aggravating the angry pounding deep in his skull, somewhere between his ears and just north of the back of his neck.

It felt like an angry little man was smashing cymbals together in there.

"I'll buy you a drink if you'll hold it down, partner."

Loco stopped laughing. "Looks like I better buy you one. You don't look so good. Them banditos do this to you? Funny they didn't kill you, eh?"

"A señorita did this to me," Longarm said.

Loco scowled, incredulous. "A girl? Don't tell me a girl killed them banditos layin' out in the street in front of my place!"

"No, I did that." Longarm looked at Loco, who was leaning forward against the bed's brass frame. "*Your* place?"

"Sure, I own this place. Cantina de Loco. Yeah, I know—the sign blew down several years ago. The wind out here—she can really blow, brother! Didn't see no reason to put it back up. Most folks know the name of the place. I was the first one in the village when gold was found in Coronado Gulch. I'm the last one here. Folks still use the road through the village, though, so I make a few pesos off the travelers. Mostly prospectors and banditos. But when I saw Sandoval comin' through my spyglass, I pulled out. Grabbed a rucksack and pulled my picket pin. Been up in the mountains livin' on mescal and roasted armadillo. I got no truck with that wildcat!"

Longarm wrinkled his nose. So that's what had fouled Loco's breath. Armadillo and mescal. He could still smell it from four feet away.

The Mexican frowned in disbelief at Longarm. "Really? You took that whole gang down?"

"Really."

"Not much left of 'em, but the wolves had left enough of Sandoval—I could tell it was him."

"Wolves gotta eat, too." Longarm had dropped his feet to the floor and was trying to get up the gumption to rise and endure the pounding that would surely increase in his poor, battered noggin.

He wondered what she'd slipped him. He'd been hungover before, but this was no normal hangover.

"Really?" Loco said. "A señorita did this to you?"

Longarm sighed. He really didn't feel like chinning about his foolishness. "Yeah, really."

"She fuck you and then tied you up? That musta been

one big señorita. You're a big man to go along with that Mexican mule dick, brother!" Loco laughed again too loudly for Longarm's tender head.

"She must've put something in the mescal we were drinking. Your good stuff."

"Ha! That's a joke. I don't have no good stuff. My mescal comes from the sisters at San Vincente, the mission school just north of here. They come sellin' that rotgut twice a month in their rickety old wagon. Wicked little pinched-up women—two parts diamondback to three parts black widow every one of 'em. But they only charge a peso a bottle, so what the hell? The old desert rats seem to like the mescal. Crave it, in fact. I buy it for them, sell it just to them."

Loco went over and picked the half-empty bottle off the dresser. There was no label on it. The cork sat beside the bottle. Loco sniffed the bottle's lip, drew his head back sharply, made a face, and closed his eyes. "Yeah, that's the stuff, all right. The Nectar of El Diablo. Boy, you shouldn't be drinkin' that stuff if you're not used to it!"

"Thanks for the warning." One of Sandoval's men must have sampled the mescal and deemed it deadly. So Claudia had just naturally thought it would kill or at least incapacitate Longarm. Which it had. And she'd made off with the army loot.

Smart little saucy bitch. When he tracked her down, he was going to spank her bare bottom and make her drink as much mescal as she'd made him drink last night. Now that he thought back on it, he couldn't remember her taking a single sip. No wonder!

Her bare bottom. Even now, after what she'd done to him, remembering her bare bottom and the sweetness of her pussy, which he'd buried his face in several times last night to lick like a frosting bowl, still made his chafed dick nod its head.

"You don't look so good, gringo lawman," Loco said with a sigh. "You'd better get something in your stomach. I'll go down and whip you up some huevos rancheros. On the house. I'd rather do that than dig a grave!"

The dark little man went out. Longarm heaved himself to his feet, having to grab a bedpost to keep from falling as the room swirled around him. He muttered, "No . . . no time for . . . huevos rancheros. Gotta get after that devilish little filly."

But he knew even as he was saying it that he'd need a little time to recover from his near-death sleep. He also needed some food in his belly. His insides felt as though they'd been soaked in acid. He imagined maggots clinging to his intestines, eating him from the inside out.

How in the hell did the old prospectors drink that stuff?

Slowly, stumbling over his own feet and wincing against the throbbing in his head, he gathered his clothes and dressed. He was surprised to find that his Colt was still in its holster and that his rifle lay atop the dresser, where he'd placed it the night before. If Claudia had taken a gun, she must have taken one of the pistols or rifles from downstairs. She must have been so sure of Longarm's demise, or at least of his long-term incapacitation, that she hadn't bothered to relieve him of his weapons.

Longarm wrapped his pistol around his waist, donned his hat, grabbed his rifle, and went downstairs. He felt better by the time he'd made the top of the stairs, though going down with the feeling that his feet were made of air was vexing.

He definitely needed some food in his belly. His stomach sort of rebelled at the smell of cooking beans coming from the other side of the curtain behind the bar, but he'd have to force Loco's breakfast down before he dared hit the trail. Without food and water, he wouldn't last an hour out in the desert.

Claudia would be easy to run down after all that rain. Her tracks would be clearly stamped in the desert sand and mud. She might even have gotten trapped by a flooded arroyo a few miles from the village. If that were the case, Longarm would have her . . . and the stolen money . . . back in no time. He didn't know what he'd do to her once he found her. He really had no legal recourse, since he was down here in Mexico illegally.

He grinned as he kicked a chair out from a table and eased himself into it. He had a vision of raising that dress above her pretty pink ass and spanking her bottom raw before sending her on home to her dear old dad and the pimply-faced kid she was doomed to marry.

Served her right having to marry some limp-dicked little fancy-steve. What better torture for a girl with her ravenous sexual cravings than to be married to a pansy?

Longarm plucked a cheroot from his pocketful of the outlaws' cigars, but before he could light it he realized how thirsty he was. He went outside to a rain barrel and drank down three dippers full of fresh water. He poured another one over his head. Curious as to which direction Claudia had headed, he tramped around out in the foggy, damp street.

It wasn't hard to pick up her trail curving out from the livery barn doors, which she'd left open in her haste to flee. She'd cut south between a couple of the abandoned buildings, her horse's shod hoof tracks plain as day.

Feeling fatigued from his ill health and the uncharacteristically humid, post-storm air, Longarm went back inside and sank down in his chair. As he was scratching a match to life on the table, Loco came out with a smoking enamel tin coffeepot and a heavy stone mug. He set the wonderful-smelling brew and the mug on the table before Longarm, looked down at the gringo lawman, winced, wagged his head, and then retreated back through the curtained doorway.

"Christ, I look that bad?" Longarm grumbled as he filled the mug with steaming black coffee.

He had to admit that as bad as he felt, he probably didn't look so good. The water had cooled him off, but he could feel a cold sweat oozing out of his skin. He felt hot then cold then hot then cold all over again.

His intestines felt like sick worms writhing in agony under his cartridge belt.

Christ, he was going to spank her raw!

Loco pushed through the curtained doorway with a steaming platter in his hands. He came around the bar and set the plate down in front of Longarm, saying, "Here we go, gringo lawman. Better eat up, brother. We gotta get some color back in your cheeks!"

He laughed and disappeared. Longarm stared down at the plate. The sick worms in his belly recoiled at the sight and smell of the four eggs topping a sprawling mound of pinto beans and jalapeño peppers covered in green gravy. But the hollowness surrounding the worms compelled him to pick up his knife and fork and to start eating.

He started slowly, washing each bite down with a sip of the coffee. He'd be damned if after the first few bites, each of which he had to swallow hard to keep down, that little bastard wielding the sledgehammer against his tender brain didn't slow down a little. He continued eating, and the worms seemed to stop writhing quite so violently.

With the beans, eggs, and coffee, his strength was returning.

He was going to live!

But then hooves pounded in the street outside. He looked through the dusty front windows to see a dozen or so riders stop in front of the hotel, their fine-lined Arabian horses stomping in place, necks and tails arched. The riders were all dressed in the bright, billowy, silver-trimmed attire of Mexican vaqueros.

Several of the riders hipped around in their saddles, obviously appraising the bloody remains of Sandoval's men still strewn about the street fronting the hotel.

Apprehension caused the worms in Longarm's gut to start writhing again when he saw the men, led by an old, gray-haired but lean and straight-backed gent, dismount their horses and mount the hotel porch.

Boots stomped and spurs rang raucously.

Loco was walking slowly, cautiously through the curtained doorway behind the bar when the hotel's front door burst open. The old gent stomped into the room, sticking out his bony chest like a rooster.

He took four long strides into the room, stopped, spread his fancily stitched black boots, and planted his gloved fists on his hips, sliding his imperious brown eyes from

Longarm to Loco and back again and announcing in Spanish, "I am Don Ernesto Franco y Anaya Cordova, and I am here searching for my daughter and I do not intend to leave here until I've found her!"

"Ah, shit," Longarm said, and dropped his fork.

Chapter 7

The old don scowled at Longarm. "Shit? Did you say '*shit*,' señor?"

Another, younger man, dressed more gaudily than any of the others, pushed through the small crowd of men to stand behind the don and glance from Longarm to Loco and back again.

"Shit?" the young man said in English. "Did someone say 'shit'?"

The old don, who wore a carefully trimmed gray beard and had a mole on the nub of his left cheek, turned his scowl on the young man and said, "Settle down, Adriano! I will handle this!"

The young man—a little taller than the don and dressed all in red and black and green and wearing a silver-trimmed black sombrero on his black-haired, shiny-faced head—frowned indignantly but said nothing. A couple of the vaqueros flanking the don looked at the younger man and snickered.

Don Cordova strode forward and stopped at Longarm's table, looking down at the federal lawman as though at horse plop he'd discovered on his polished walnut floor and which the servants had been remiss in not scooping up. "Did you say 'shit,' señor?"

Longarm casually sipped his coffee and leaned back in his chair. "Yeah. Talkin' to myself. Shit, I ate too damn much." He feigned a wince and pressed a hand to his belly. "Gonna get loggy here soon."

The don carefully, suspiciously scrutinized the big man sitting slouched before him.

"All right, so you have eaten too much. Perhaps you might wish to answer my question. I am looking for my daughter. She was in the hands of that *pendejo* Sandoval and his unwashed border banditos. I see that most of them are now outside, dead in the street, their guts appropriately strewn. What about my daughter, Claudia Anna Cordova?"

"That her name?"

"That is her name!" intoned the young, shiny-faced man, who Longarm assumed was Claudia's soon-to-be-husband. He didn't have many pimples, but if you took away his height of around six feet, he'd look like a twelve-year-old boy under that big sombrero. A spoiled, pampered, mean-eyed, prissy twelve-year-old boy.

"Have you seen her?" Young Lorca jerked his chin toward the old man as he said, "She has been promised to me by Don Cordova, and I swear if anyone has touched a hair on her head—!"

"Adriano!" the don shouted. "You will defer to me or I will send you back to the hacienda. I am Don Cordova. I am in charge here. I will ask the questions. Now, go wait outside with the horses before you make me angry and regret as well as reconsider promising my dear Claudia to you!"

Adriano's pale cheeks turned beet-red. He scowled at Longarm, nostrils flaring. He brushed a hand across the pearl grips of the silver-plated .45 he wore in a hand-tooled leather holster on his left hip, and then ground his jaws together, wheeled, pushed through the vaqueros clumped between the don and the door, and out onto the veranda.

"Kind of a hothead, ain't he?" Longarm asked the don.

"Who are you, señor?"

"Me?" Longarm said. "I'm just driftin' through."

"I see. Well, Señor Drifting Through, are you responsible for the dead men I see in the street?"

"Me?" Longarm glanced at Loco. "Hell, no. You see what happened was there was another gang here, and the gang that was here before Sandoval showed up *bushwhacked Sandoval*."

"Bushwhacked?" The don's wiry gray brows furled worriedly over his rheumy, copper eyes. "And . . . my daughter . . . ?"

"Bushwhackers took her." Longarm cut his eyes to Loco, who quirked a mouth corner. "Headed east. Straight east. All this was before the rain, so you'll have a devil of a time trackin' 'em, but east is where they headed all right. With your daughter. Ain't that right, Señor Loco?"

Loco tensed, startled. "East. *Sí, sí*, Don Cordova." He gave his chin a respectful dip. "East is the direction in which they took your daughter."

"When?" the don barked, anxious to get moving.

"Yesterday before the rain hit," Longarm told him, relighting his half-smoked cigar.

The don scowled down at the lawman whose head was ensconced in billowing clouds of cigar smoke, the match flame leaping at the end of the cheroot.

"Who are you, señor?" Cordova asked, narrowing a skeptical eye.

"Me?" Longarm said, smiling smugly up at the man. He had a natural aversion to men with power. Especially arrogant men with power. "I told ya. I'm just drifting through."

"You do know I could have a better answer whipped out of you."

"Oh, sure, you could," Longarm said, glancing at the well-armed vaqueros clumped behind the older man. "But your daughter and them owlhoots that grabbed her would get just all that much farther from here, wouldn't they?"

The don flared his nostrils. His narrow chest rose and fell slowly, heavily. "We will meet again, señor."

"I doubt it," Longarm said. "Me? I'm headed back north. Be across the border by sundown, most likely."

The don spit out a wicked Spanish curse, wheeled, and shouted at his men, who jerked to life and fairly ran back out of the hotel and into the street. The don followed. A minute later, only the dwindling rumble of their galloping horses remained to say they had ever been there. By the time the rumbling was gone, Longarm had grabbed his Winchester and was running to the livery barn on the other side of the street.

He saddled his brindle bay, filled two canteens at a rain barrel, and stuffed his Winchester down into his saddle sheath. He mounted up and rode the bay out of the barn and into the still-muddy street, over which the fog was dwindling to vapor snakes writhing over the puddles. Loco stood on the hotel's porch, filling a pipe.

"Señor Longarm, do you realize you told a lie to Don Cordova?" he called.

"What about it?" Longarm asked, angling his horse after the girl's tracks.

Loco hiked a shoulder. "Very bad, Longarm. He will be very angry when he realizes you sent him off in the wrong direction."

"He'll get over it," Longarm shouted as he put the brindle between the two abandoned shacks.

"Oh, I don't think so!" Loco called behind him. More faintly, the man's voice yelled, "The don can be a very angry and dangerous man, Señor Longarm!"

"Yeah, well, so can I," Longarm growled.

Claudia Cordova reined her cream Arabian stallion to a halt atop a low hill. She stared down the hill ahead of her. Just beyond the hill's bottom, a broad arroyo curved from her left to her right, between her and a steep-sided sandstone ridge.

The arroyo was flooded. Butterscotch-colored water rose to its banks. The flotsam on the water slid quickly down the arroyo. She could hear the murmur of the water against its banks from where she sat atop the hill.

The water was moving fast. The hair rose on the back of the señorita's neck. It looked deep. Deep and fast, making crossing it perilous business indeed.

Damn the rainstorm!

She glanced along her back trail. No movement among those rocky hills, sun-bleached bluffs, and shelving mesas.

Not so much as a bird or a coyote. So why did she have the uneasy feeling she was being watched and followed?

She wished now she'd had the nerve to kill Longarm. But she hadn't. She'd never killed a man before, much less one who'd pleased her so thoroughly.

She splayed her hand between her legs. She could still feel the hammering of the lawman's cock in her pussy, plundering her core and fulfilling every nook and cranny of her womanhood with his brusque yet somehow gentle masculinity. She'd been deflowered years ago by her father's *segundo*, now long dead, and she had frolicked many times since without her father ever finding out. If he'd known how many men she'd been with—twenty at least!—he'd likely have slit her throat and then hunted down each of the hombres who'd rutted with her and doled out the same justice to him.

That's the kind of man Don Cordova was. He'd rather kill his beloved Claudia than allow her to live in disgrace. And he'd kill any many who'd disgraced her. She was his only daughter, after all.

Claudia wished she'd been able to kill Longarm, but perhaps the liquor had killed him. Sandoval had drunk a glass of it and promptly lost his head and tried to rape Claudia. She'd grown so horny being around so many rough, masculine characters that she probably would have allowed herself to be savaged.

But before the bandito leader had been able to do the dirty deed, he'd passed out, leaving Claudia frustrated.

Longarm had come along at just the right moment.

He'd drunk nearly half the bottle of mescal while fucking her with his wonderful staff. Perhaps he was indeed dead and she could stop worrying.

Still . . .

She gazed cautiously along her back trail once more, apprehension drawing the muscles taut between her shoulder blades.

She turned back to the arroyo. Deep and wide as it looked, she had to get across.

She booted her Arab on down the hill and stopped at the edge of the gurgling water. The arroyo was about fifty yards across. She couldn't tell how deep the water was, but she'd have bet that her horse couldn't stand up in it.

Claudia touched the spurred heels of her riding boots to the Arabian's ribs. The horse dutifully stepped off the bank and plunged with a snorting grunt into the water.

Claudia glanced back at the saddlebags bulging with the American greenbacks. Quickly, before the water could close over the tops of the bags, she scooped them off the Arab's rear end and draped them over her left shoulder, holding them up above the swirling surface of the water.

The Arabian heaved itself forward in the current pushing against it from the left. The current slid horse and rider downstream several yards, but even so, the stalwart, well-trained stallion made progress toward the other side.

Claudia heaved a sigh of relief when she could feel the horse gaining its footing. The bank on this side of the arroyo was steeper than the one she'd left, but the horse saw a notch in the bank rising among willows, and headed for it. It gained the notch, paused for a quick breather, and then lunged up the bank by way of the notch. It clomped through the willows and stopped so suddenly that Claudia was almost thrown over the mount's fine head.

She gasped when she saw what had startled the stallion.

Four unshaven men in grubby clothes and battered sombreros sat four horses not ten feet in front of her, facing her, blocking her path.

They all stared at her, eyes bright with lust as they took in her curvaceous frame poorly concealed by the tight-fitting dress under which she wasn't wearing any underwear. She found underwear too hot and confining, so she hadn't taken long to shed it once she'd ridden away from her father's hacienda.

The man sitting a blaze-faced black glanced at the other men to each side of him, whistled his appreciation of the señorita before him, and said in Spanish, "Now, that, *mi amigos*, is a sight for sore eyes, is it not?"

Claudia pulled the big pistol she'd wedged behind the belt holding her dress closed. It was a heavy piece—too heavy for her, but she had been able to find no lighter revolvers among the guns back at the hotel in which she'd left the lawman tied and unconscious. She pulled the hammer back, wincing at the effort.

"You just stay right there!" she ordered. "Stay right there or I'll shoot!"

"Stay right here?" asked the man who'd whistled at her. "When there is soo much woman over *there?*"

"*Sí*, but that woman has a pistol," Claudia warned, her voice quaking.

"A very big pistol," said the man on the group's far right.

He had only one eye. A nasty scar twisted his mouth, framed by long mare's-tail mustaches. He had a big revolver hanging from a thong around his neck. "Maybe too much pistol for the señorita, no?"

He gave a wild yell and kicked his horse forward.

Claudia screamed and involuntarily squeezed the hammer of the gun in her hands. The pistol exploded, leaping out of her hands as though it were a frightened animal. At the same time, she saw the man with the scarred lip go rolling off the back of his horse.

She didn't see the wounded gent hit the ground, because then her own stallion reared sharply, whinnying shrilly, and suddenly she was falling back off the stallion's butt. She caught a glimpse of the saddlebags tumbling to the ground near a barrel cactus.

A quarter second later, she hit the ground hard enough to scramble her brains.

She was vaguely aware of rolling, rolling back down the notch. And then the cool wetness of the flooded arroyo closed over her, and the unseen hands of the current were pulling and pushing her downstream.

Chapter 8

Longarm rode up to the top of a low hill and stopped his brindle bay about twenty yards down the other side. A minute ago, he'd thought he heard voices on the wind. He heard them again now—a man or men speaking loudly. He thought he could hear the occasional, higher strains of a woman's voice, as well.

Now he could hear the woman's voice more clearly.

On the other side of a flooded arroyo and a couple of low, rocky, willow-stippled hills, dust rose in the brassy, afternoon desert light. The men and the woman or women were scuffling around.

Longarm gave a wry snort and ground his heels against the bay's flanks. He galloped over to the edge of the arroyo and inspected the water. He briefly considered looking for a shallower place to cross, but then the woman screamed, and he shelved the idea. He batted his heels against the bay's flanks, and suddenly he and the horse were in the tepid water, sliding downstream while the horse lunged and jerked, snorting desperately, toward the other side.

The yells, screams, and dust were rising from about a hundred yards downstream. Longarm was growing worried that the bay might let the current sweep him on past the scene of the dustup and possibly into view of those to whom the voices belonged. But then the horse's head jerked up. His hooves found purchase on the arroyo's bottom. The water slid down Longarm's legs and then the horse gave a grunt as he started lunging up the far bank.

The lawman stopped the horse among clay-colored boulders about twenty yards beyond the arroyo, and slipped out of the saddle. He tied the bay to a branch, shucked his Winchester '73 from the leather scabbard, and quietly pumped a round into the chamber.

Looking around, he found what appeared to be a game path through the boulders, and began following it on a parallel course with the arroyo. As he walked, tracing a serpentine course through the brush, cacti, and rocks, the voices were growing louder. They belonged to one girl and at least two men, possibly three, maybe four. They were all speaking Spanish. Because she was speaking Spanish instead of English, Longarm couldn't be certain, but he was pretty sure the girl's voice belonged to the black-hearted beauty he had been following since the morning.

Keying on the voices, Longarm stepped a little farther away from the arroyo, threaded a natural corridor between large, flat-topped, cabin-sized boulders, and dropped to a knee.

He was on a rise overlooking a sandy clearing rimmed with more rocks and cacti. In the clearing below him were four people. Three of the people were men in ragged trail garb and frayed sombreros.

Banditos. Probably the particularly nasty brand that haunted these mountains, on the run, most likely, from American posses.

The fourth person was Claudia Cordova.

She was naked and wet and sand clung to her knees and the tips of her breasts and to her chin, as though she'd recently fallen. The sun shone like copper on her glistening tan body with its full, rich, upturned breasts. Her wet hair hung down past her shoulders, with a couple of chestnut curls pasted to the sides of her tits, which jostled as she waved a gray chunk of driftwood at two of the men, who were facing her, trying to get close to her.

While Claudia held the two men back with the chunk of driftwood, a third man sat on a rock at the side of the clearing to Longarm's left. The third man had the moneybags draped over his thighs. Packets of greenbacks were spilled on the ground around his boots. He was counting one of the packets now, grinning around the cigar poking out of one corner of his mouth.

"I'm warning, you," Claudia screamed in Spanish at the two men toying with her, laughing and lunging and then darting back when she swung the driftwood at them. "I am Claudia Cordova. Daughter of Don Cordova, and if any of you tries to stick his rancid dick in me, my father will hunt you down and have you drawn and quartered!"

She glanced toward the man counting the army loot. "And that's my money, you bastard!"

Just then one of the two men nearest her leaped behind her and grabbed her around the waist. Picking her up off the ground, kicking and screaming, he fondled her breasts and nuzzled her neck. Claudia tried to club him with the wood in her hand, but he merely slashed at her flailing arm, and the wood tumbled to the ground.

The man facing her told the other man to hold her tight, that he was going to turn her into a woman. Longarm didn't have the heart to tell the bandito that Claudia Cordova had likely been a woman for longer than the bandito had been a man. They all seemed so enthralled with their prize.

Two prizes.

The beautiful, wet, naked girl and the mother lode of American money she had brought them.

Longarm hunkered down behind a barrel cactus and doffed his hat. He thumbed the Winchester's hammer back to full cock.

In the clearing below, the bandito who'd said he was going to make Claudia a woman was shedding his cartridge belt and three holstered pistols while the other man seemed to be thoroughly enjoying himself, fondling Claudia's breasts and nuzzling her neck. The girl was sobbing and raging and flailing futilely at her primary attacker.

He was a big man—big and broad and powerful. She almost looked the size of a doll in his giant arms, pulled back against his massive chest. He guffawed as he ravaged her.

"Hold her good now, Tio!" said the other man, who'd unbuttoned his pants and was approaching Claudia now, cock jutting. "I'm going to really give it to her! No man will be enough for her after I get done with her!"

"Just hurry up and fuck her, Ramon!" Tio growled. "Then it's *my* turn!"

Longarm looked at the third man. He was now reaching down for one of the packets scattered around his boots. The lawman had to hurry before he looked up again.

He snaked the Winchester around the right side of the barrel cactus. Big Tio was facing Longarm's direction, but he was much too preoccupied with the beautiful woman in his arms to look up the rise in front of him. Ramon had hold of Claudia's bare legs and was lifting them, stepping between them, preparing to mount the struggling girl.

His back was to Longarm. Longarm had no trouble shooting Ramon in the back. Ramon deserved much worse. What did trouble the lawman, however, was the possibility that he might miss Ramon, who was shuffling around as he mounted Claudia, and hit the girl he was trying to save.

But, then again, how worried did he really need to be? He reflected on his waking earlier that morning to find himself tied, naked and spread-eagled, to the bed in Loco's hotel, and on the continuing ache in his head and his general, overall fatigue from the mescal poison still coursing through his veins and oozing out his pores.

Longarm gave a caustic chuff as he snapped the Winchester's butt plate to his right shoulder, aimed hastily, and squeezed the trigger.

The rifle belched loudly, echoing flatly.

Ramon's head jerked forward. His body followed a second later, and he fell against Tio and Claudia. As Tio stumbled back away from the suddenly brainless Tio, the big bandito spread his arms and gaped in shock at the vaporized brains and blood covering his face and upper chest and shoulders.

Longarm's Winchester spoke again, drilling a large, round hole in the middle of big Tio's forehead. Tio dropped as though someone had clubbed the back of his knees. As the big Mexican and Ramon lay jerking with death spasms, Longarm pumped a fresh round into the Winchester's action and swung the rifle to his left.

The third man tossed the money he'd been counting to the ground and gained his feet, filling his fists with two big horse pistols. He managed to squeeze off a shot before Longarm could draw a bead on him. The bullet smashed into the rock just left of Longarm's face, spraying rock shards and nudging the lawman's own bullet wide.

Longarm blinked, wincing against the bee-like sting of a shard in his cheek, then seated and fired another round. That slug plumed dirt behind the third Mex, who'd taken off running away from the clearing. When he paused and swung around and fired both his pistols, both bullets hammering the boulders well wide of Longarm now, the lawman took a second and a half to plant a bead on his chest and send his heart flying out his back in shreds clinging to bits of spine and gobs of blood.

He twisted around wildly, fell, rolled onto his back, groaning, and crossed his ankles as though he'd just lain down for a nap. He shook as though he'd been struck by lightning, before gradually settling down into the peacefulness of death. Longarm heard him fart.

The lawman glanced around, making sure there no other banditos nearby, and then climbed down out of the rocks, cat-footed down the steep slope, and strode over to where Claudia Cordova lay belly down near big Tio and Ramon, who also lay belly down, blood oozing out the hole in the back of his head.

Claudia had her arms up over her head and was shaking and moaning. "*Por favor,*" she said, "don't kill me. Oh, please don't kill me." She rolled over onto her back, showing her breasts that were splattered with Ramon's blood and brains and bits of skull, and wiped some of the same substance off her left cheek. "I will give you anything you want. Anything. I am a rich woman, you know. I will share my . . ."

Claudia blinked up at Longarm, squinting against the sun kiting across the sky behind him. He rested his rifle on his shoulder and pulled one of Sandoval's cheroots from the breast pocket of his frock coat.

"Oh, my god," the señorita said, her voice pitched with awe. "*Longarm?*"

The lawman scratched a lucifer to life on his holster and touched the flame to the cheroot protruding straight out from his teeth.

"My god, Longarm!" Claudia's eyes brightened. She climbed to her feet, smiling, showing all those beautiful teeth though her face was less than beautiful at the moment, speckled as it was with Ramon's brains and blood. "My god, Longarm!" she repeated, louder, and ran toward him, throwing her arms wide as if to hug him. "I was so worried I'd killed you! Oh, you have no idea how much I have regretted—!"

She stopped abruptly when Longarm lowered his rifle from his shoulder and planted the end of the barrel against her chest, in the deep cleavage between her goo-splattered tits. He drew more smoke into his lungs and blew it at her. She blinked against it, waving a hand in front of her face, frowning.

"Longarm, truly I am sorry—"

"You're a damn mess. Best get yourself cleaned up, get ready to ride." Longarm jerked his chin in the direction of the flooded arroyo.

"You are angry," she said.

"Where's your horse?"

"I don't know. Over there . . . somewhere." She waved her arm carelessly.

"Like I said," Longarm repeated, blowing more smoke at her. "Best get yourself cleaned up. Be ready to ride in fifteen minutes. We'll be pullin' out."

Claudia turned away from him, choking softly on his smoke. She glanced over her shoulder at him, looking like a little girl who didn't get the puppy she'd wanted for Christmas, and continued tramping naked, head down, toward the arroyo, steering her bare feet wide of cactus patches.

In spite of his disdain for the girl, he couldn't help admiring the fineness of her body. At the moment, however, he was more concerned about the stolen money than Claudia's irresistible ass.

Quickly, he gathered up all the packets, stuffed them into the saddlebags, buckled the flaps down tight over the pouches, and slung the bags over his left shoulder, leaving his right arm free for his Winchester. He glanced once more toward the flooded arroyo, where he could hear Claudia splashing as she cleaned herself, though he could not see her from here.

He sighed, ignored the strong male pull of the girl in his crotch, tugged his hat brim low, rolled the cigar from one corner of his mouth to the other, and tramped off through the rocks for his horse. When he found the brindle bay where he'd left it, he secured the saddlebags over his own bags, behind the cantle of his saddle, and mounted up, heading off in search of Claudia's horse.

Doing so, he found whom he took to be a fourth bandito, lying dead at the mouth of a notch that led down to the water. The dead man sported a bullet hole in his left temple. Longarm gave a snort and continued his search for the Arab, which he found a good fifty yards from the arroyo, cropping galetta grass in a stand of spindly sycamores and cottonwoods.

It took the lawman some time to ease up close enough to the nervous Arab so he could grab its dangling reins, but he managed to lead the horse back into the clearing where the three dead men lay just as Claudia was walking back from the creek, pulling her dress around her wet shoulders and tying the belt at her waist. Her wet hair hung straight down past her shoulders, several thick strands dancing across her cleavage.

Longarm didn't doubt that she'd arranged it that way.

He gave her a disgusted scowl as he dismounted and tied the horses to a willow near where the third bandito lay atop his shredded heart that was splattered across a century plant. Claudia stood regarding the tall lawman coyly, twisting a lock of her damp hair around her finger. Her body was still wet behind the dress, which clung to her enticingly. Her distended nipples pushed against the cloth.

The expression on her chiseled, brown-eyed face was one of coy bemusement. "You don't look so good," she said. "You look a little pale, amigo."

Longarm removed the cigar from his mouth and studied the coal. "Yeah, well, I'm feelin' fit as a fiddle."

"What are you going to do with me?" Sneering, she

shook her hair back behind her shoulder. "Don't forget who I am. The daughter of Don Cordova. Down here, where you have no business being, gringo lawman, that name means something. It means more than something. You lay one hand on me, my father will hunt you down and have you gelded."

She said this last with emphasis, jerking her chin up at him and sort of spitting "gelded" out like a prune pit.

Longarm smacked her across her right cheek with the back of his hand. She went tumbling in a cloud of dust.

Chapter 9

"Bastard!" Claudia cried, glaring up at him through her mussed wet hair, bare legs curled beneath her on the ground. Her dress had come open, revealing both her beautiful, tan breasts.

"You asked for one hell of a lot more than that," Longarm grumbled as he walked past her. "So be glad it's all you got . . . so far."

"Where are you going?"

"Shut up."

Longarm climbed up into some rocks on the west end of the clearing. He dropped to a knee between two of the rocks and looked over the flooded arroyo, which was going down only gradually as the water from last night's storm rushed out of the higher mountains. Beyond the arroyo lay several chalky bluffs tufted with cactus and greasewood. He was peering between two of these buttes and along his back trail, when hooves clomped below and to his left.

Claudia was straddling her Arabian, grinning snidely up at Longarm as the horse pranced toward the water. "Good-bye, lawman! I've decided to let you keep the money since you seem so heartbroken without it. I'll be going now! Hope you're not too lonely without meee!"

Longarm pinched his hat brim to her and curled one corner of his mouth. Claudia put the Arab into the arroyo with a splash, and the horse began swimming toward the other side. Longarm watched as horse and rider gained the opposite bank. Atop the bank, Claudia turned the horse, looked back toward Longarm, blew him a jeering kiss, and waved.

Longarm grinned and waved back to her.

Claudia turned the horse away from the arroyo and booted it into a trot. As they threaded the crease between the buttes, the girl booted the fine Arabian into a lope. They turned around the backside of the right butte and disappeared.

Longarm relit his cigar, rolled it from one corner of his mouth to the other as he stared after the girl, and drew several deep puffs of peppery Mexican tobacco smoke into his lungs. He watched and waited, holding the rifle barrel up in his right hand, the stock resting on a small rock before him.

He caressed the hammer with his gloved right thumb.

Shortly, a man shouted off to the east, in the direction Longarm was gazing. Another man shouted, as well, and then one gave a raucous whoop while yet another imitated a jubilant coyote. A girl's scream careened through the desert mountain quiet, and presently hooves thumped madly.

A few seconds later, Claudia and the Arab reappeared, galloping back into the crease between the buttes from the other side, dashing toward Longarm. The girl leaned forward, crouching over the horse's arched neck as she rammed her riding boots into the Arab's flanks, urging more speed.

She glanced behind her as five riders came around the backside of the right butte, galloping hard and whooping and hollering and whistling and one doing a damn good imitation of a love-struck coyote. Two of the five riders were dressed much like the three Longarm had killed earlier.

Two of the other three were dressed like gringos, in Stetsons and vests over calico shirts, bandannas knotted around their necks. The fifth man appeared to be a half-breed. He wore a red bandanna around his forehead, and his long, black hair whipped behind him in the wind. He rode with a rifle standing barrel-up on his thigh, and a knife handle was visible as well.

The five were a sunburned, unshaven lot with many guns flashing in the brassy afternoon sun.

A mixed bag of border bandits. In other words, banditos of the worst stripe.

Claudia screamed and booted her Arab on into the arroyo. The men behind her were closing on her fast.

"Longarm!" Claudia cried. "Please help me!"

"Why should I?" Longarm growled under his breath, grinning toward the oncoming riders.

"Longarm!" Claudia screamed when, looking over her shoulder, she saw the pack of wild riders approaching the arroyo.

One of the two Mexicans drew a revolver and extended it toward Claudia, his teeth showing a white line beneath his thick black mustache. Longarm snapped his Winchester up and shot the Mexican out of his saddle.

As the Mexican hit the ground with a groan and rolled

wildly, dust rising, the other five riders snapped their heads toward Longarm and sawed back on their horse's reins. The horses skidded to dusty halts on the bank of the arroyo.

Longarm plunked three more .44 rounds into the water at the far edge of the arroyo, two feet in front of the girl's pursuers. As the bullets plumed the mud-brown water, the five riders jerked their horses around and beat it back through the crease down which they had come, leaving their fallen comrade piled up on a patch of Spanish bayonet, unmoving. The dead man's horse followed them, trailing its bridle reins.

Claudia's Arab climbed the near bank and shook mud from its coat. Claudia looked back to see her pursuers disappearing behind the right butte. She scowled up at Longarm, jaws hard, teeth gritted.

"You knew they were back there!"

"Yeah, they been doggin' my trail for the past hour. I figured they were out to rob me. Probably got a better idea when they saw you." Longarm grinned.

"Why did you not tell me, you bastard?"

Longarm pushed himself to his feet and started negotiating the rocks back toward the clearing in which the three dead men lay. "Plum forgot," he lied, and then leaped the last few feet from the rocky slope to the ground.

He adjusted the saddlebags on his shoulder, puffed the cigar in his teeth, grinned at the scowling girl once more, and strode back to his horse.

Later, as Longarm and Claudia rode west through the high desert mountains under a furnace-like sun, she said, "Well, what are your big plans for me, huh, *pendejo?* If you think you have any recourse down here, you are badly mistaken. Even if anyone believed that I, Claudia Cordova, daughter of . . ."

"Daughter of the great Don Cordova, I remember," Longarm filled in for her.

"*Sí*—if anyone believed that the daughter of Don Cordova stole that stolen money, and that is a *muy* big *if*, amigo, you must remember that it is gringo money, and no one down here in *my home* country of Mexico would give a rat's ass about stolen gringo greenbacks!"

Riding on Longarm's right, she glanced at him with a mock-serious frown. "Besides, are you even down here *legally*, gringo, *pendejo* lawman? Or could you possibly even be hanged if anyone in official authority discovered that you were here, pestering, even *raping* the pure, virginal daughters of rich, respected Mexican dons?"

Longarm laughed and looked at her, astonished. "*Rape? You're* more guilty of raping *me* than *I* am of raping *you,* my dear señorita*!*"

"Tell that to the Rurales! Tell that to *mi papa!*"

"You little wench," Longarm snarled. "I should have let them outlaws back there catch you and have their ways with you."

She cast him a sly smile. "Maybe you were jealous, huh?"

"Doubtful."

Claudia hipped around in her saddle to stare worriedly along their back trail. "I am much woman, Longarm. As you yourself know so well. I think you should have killed them all when you had the chance. They will follow, I assure you."

"Oh, I reckon they will. And you're likely right—I should have gone ahead and blown each one out of his saddle rather than just sprinkle down a little warnin'. Trouble is, I have a hard time shootin' men from ambush. Even ones out to stake a girl out in the desert and take turns violating her with their disease-ridden peckers."

Claudia glared at him. "Do you have to make it so vivid?"

Longarm gave a rueful snort.

"So," Claudia said, "what are your plans for me?"

Longarm glanced at the cactus-bristling desert behind them. "If I hadn't picked them up, and if I didn't think they were still trailin' us, I'd have let you ride on back to your old man's hacienda. Believe me, I don't want you in my hair any more than you want me in yours. But I figure leaving you to your own devices would be damn near equal to murder. Unless . . ."

Longarm glanced once more over his shoulder.

"Unless what?" she said, indignant.

"Unless your old man shows up."

"My *old man?*"

"Yeah, him and your promised one showed up at Loco's place when I was just pullin' out. They were trailin' you. Since I didn't want them catchin' up to you before I did, and before I could confiscate the money you so rudely stole from me after poisoning, fucking, and hog-tying me, I sent them on a wild goose chase."

"Longarm!"

He turned to her. She regarded him with dire beseeching in her large brown eyes. She lowered her voice as if to emphasize the graveness of her plea. "You must not return me to *mi papa*. Nor to Señor Lorca. *Por favor*, I beseech you with all my heart. I will make it very much worth your while to let me ride with you until it is safe for us to part ways. At least, safe for me to part with you."

Longarm stared at her, incredulous. "Boy, you really don't want to marry that kid, do you?"

"Please, if you promise to keep me out of their hands, tonight around a cozy campfire, I will suck your large and beautiful cock like you have never had it sucked before."

Longarm continued to stare at her. He looked at her mouth, remembered how it had felt to have it sliding up and down his love mast, and tried with all his might to let the memory go. "Well, if it's so all-fired important to you, Claudia—okay. All right. I won't haze you into the lion's den. I'd be curious to know why, but just as soon as we can get you somewhere safe, you're free to do as you please." He dropped his chin and ridged his brows in parental admonishing. "But if you were from my side of the border, you could bet the seed bull I'd be hauling you off to the nearest hoosegow pronto, you thief!"

Claudia smiled prettily and winked. "I am going to suck your cock beautifully tonight, my big gringo lawman."

Longarm turned away in disgruntlement and spat to one side. "Ah, hell."

Chapter 10

While he and Claudia rode throughout that day, Longarm tried to keep his mind off the young siren riding beside him and her large breasts jiggling inside the low-cut bodice of her skimpy dress. He tried instead to keep his mind on his back trail as well as the trail before him, to avoid run-ins with the bandits likely following him and any more who might spy him and the beautiful girl from afar.

His thoughts concerning Claudia were restricted to how in hell he was going to get away from her, how in hell he was going to get the stolen army money back across the border. By the early afternoon he had enough of a handle on the mountainous desert terrain they were riding through to remember that a fairly sizeable village lay on the range's far east side. He couldn't remember the village's name, but he did remember it had a rail line passing through from the border which connected it in a roundabout way with Mexico City.

If he could get through these harsh, rugged, banditoinfested mountains in one piece, and get to the village, he could turn the señorita free knowing that she'd be far safer being turned loose there than out here, where she'd have less of a shot at survival than a hare at a rattlesnake convention.

They followed what Longarm suspected was an old Apache or Yaqui Indian trail ever higher into the mountains, until pines and firs began rising around them. The air turned mercifully cooler. It was perfumed with the tang of pine resin and the verdant smells of creeks and streams. At one such stream, they dismounted to give their tired horses a breather, as well as water and time to crop the rich, green grass growing along the bank.

When they'd finished tending the horses, Longarm dunked his head in the stream and took a long, cold drink. Claudia did the same. "Oooo, that's so good and refreshing!" she exclaimed.

She removed her high-topped riding boots and slipped down off the bank. Holding her dress above her knees, she began wading around like a little girl on her way home from school, enjoying her freedom as well as the luxuriousness of the water against her bare legs.

Longarm slaked his thirst on the cold water until his ears rang, and then he filled their canteens. He sat on a rock in the shade of a tall pine, fished a half-smoked cigar from his pocket, and scraped a lucifer to life on his thumbnail. Claudia continued to frolic in the stream, singing softly to herself some old Spanish love ballad and kicking her beautiful legs, splashing water that the high-altitude sun painted with fleeting rainbows.

She kicked some water at Longarm, and then she climbed the low opposite bank, knelt at the water's edge, and uncinched her dress. She let it fall to her waist. She gave Longarm a mocking grin then shook her hair back and leaned forward. Her breasts slanted out from her chest as she bathed her face in the stream.

When she lifted her head, she said, "Oh, so fresh!" and shook her head. The water rained down from her face to her chest, streaking across her breasts and glistening gold in the sunshine.

Longarm sucked the quirley against the heat building in his pecker. She must have seen his desire in his eyes because she said, mocking, "A gentleman would avert his gaze."

"I reckon I ain't a gentleman," the lawman groused.

"That's for sure." She sank back on her heels, throwing her shoulders back, tits forward. They jutted toward Longarm like a matched pair of .45s. "Would you like some?"

Longarm drew another deep drag from his cigar. He tried not to glance at the tits, but he couldn't help himself. He had to resist her, however. He knew that she were trying to make him let his guard down, likely so she could grab his gun or maybe brain him with a rock and take the loot.

Blowing the smoke out on the warm breeze, he lied. "Ain't tempted in the least."

"Oh, I think you are," she said, winking and pulling the dress back up over her shoulders.

"Get back over here," he said curtly. "Time to mount up and get movin."

"Spoil sport." Claudia rose and stepped back into the stream.

While she sat down to dry her feet in the grass and

pull her boots back on, Longarm walked back up to where the horses nibbled grass and lazily switched their tails. The lawman peered down the stone- and cedar-stippled slope beyond the horses. From here he had a pretty good view of his and the señorita's back trail, the slopes rolling away toward the tan desert floor far below to the northwest.

Nothing moved in that direction except one hawk tracing a lazy circle high in the misty, light blue air over the burning desert.

He heard footsteps behind him. Claudia was climbing the slope from the creek. She paused by the Arab and ran a long-fingered hand down the horse's neck.

"See anything back there?" she asked.

"Nothin'."

"They will come."

"How do you know?" he asked her.

She gave him a knowing grin and once more shook that thick, chestnut hair back from her face. "Wouldn't you?"

Longarm chuckled as he walked over to the brindle bay and reached under the horse's belly for the latigo strap. "Miss Claudia, knowing you like I do now, I'd run in the opposite direction." He chuckled again as he tightened the cinch. "I'd run like a donkey with tin cans tied to its tail!"

"Very funny." Claudia scoffed, walking around to the Arab's left side. "When are we going to stop for the night? I'm hungry."

"I'll let you know," Longarm said, glancing over his shoulder once more, sliding his gaze across the rocky, cactus-studded knobs rolling out beyond. He was not happy with the situation. If he hadn't had to worry about her—this girl who had nearly fucked him literally to death and stolen the stolen loot he'd risked life and limb to ride down here, against the law, to secure—he could have made a beeline for the border.

If all went well, he could have been delivering the money to the U.S. marshal's office in Prescott within a week.

But no. Now he had to get this Sonora siren safely to the other side of the mountains lest she fall prey to the sort of wildcats, human and otherwise, that hid out in this rugged corner of the Sonoran desert.

"Come on," Longarm urged as he swung up onto the bay's back. "Let's shake a leg here, Claudia. I got a job to do, dammit."

"Don't be angry with me, Longarm," she said, as she swung up onto the Arab's back, pouting. She cracked another lascivious smile. "I told you—I will make it all up to you later."

"Stow it," he said, booting the bay back onto the trail.

Longarm and his unlikely charge traveled slowly eastward until the giant lemon drop of the sun was teetering precariously over the top of an arrow-shaped peak far to the west. The lawman led his trail partner into a ravine rimmed with pines and threaded by a small, chuckling brook, and there he and Claudia tended their horses and set up camp.

Longarm had pilfered food from the banditos he'd killed, including some salted beef and pinto beans, and while the food warmed in a single pan over the small fire he'd built despite the fact that the flames might be seen by the men tracking them. If the men who'd chased

Claudia were indeed tracking them. So far, Longarm had seen no sign of that, though the skin across the back of his neck had prickled on and off all day.

The sensation had saved his life far too many times for him not to recognize it for what it was—a surefire indication that the lawman's sixth sense he'd sort of semiconsciously cultivated over his long years as a badge-toter was registering trouble. Whether said trouble came from the men who'd been after Claudia earlier or from some other quarter, Longarm didn't know. It didn't really matter.

He had to keep his eyes and ears skinned and hope that he'd built the cook fire small enough and deep enough inside the ravine that it wouldn't be too easily spotted from the pine-covered slopes rising all around him.

When the beans and beef were smoking, Claudia filled two tin plates with the grub and gave one to Longarm. She filled two cups with coffee brewed from the lawman's stores and gave him one of those, as well. She sat back against a tree, crossed her long, bare legs at the ankles, gave him a dubious look from the other side of the dancing flames, and started eating.

Longarm scraped the end off his current cheroot, saving the cigar for later, and dug into his own supper. By now, it was nearly dark, and the small flames were reflected dully off the sandstone walls of the ravine, which was no more than forty or so yards wide. The brook ran along the base of the wall behind Claudia. It murmured quietly beneath the crackling of the fire.

As he ate, Longarm glanced curiously at the girl sitting across from him. When he'd finished his meal, he sat back against his saddle with a fresh cup of coffee, relit the cheroot, and said, "Tell me, Claudia—what's the real reason you don't want to go home?"

"I told you," she said, chewing and hiking a shoulder. "I have no wish to be enslaved by the likes of Adriano Lorca. I would rather *die!*"

"Ah, come on—you would not."

Claudia stopped chewing to scowl across the fire at him. Quietly, she repeated, "I would rather die than be sold to that man. Into the slavery of that sniveling little rich man."

Longarm scowled. "Chew that up a little finer, will you, Claudia? I don't think I understand. What's this about slavery?"

Claudia put her fork down on her empty plate, set the plate aside, and sat up a little, drawing her knees toward her chest and lacing her fingers around them. "Don Cordova is not really my father, Longarm. He is my master."

Longarm blinked. Blowing cigar smoke out his nose, he curled his upper lip and narrowed a skeptical eye.

"I am half-Yaqui—the daughter of an unholy union between a Mexican Rurale and a Yaqui woman—my mother. My mother was raped by the Rurale. She and my stepfather raised me with my two half sisters and one half brother. We worked on Don Cordova's hacienda, cutting hay and firewood. My father also broke wild horses."

Claudia leaned forward and used a leather swatch to lift the coffeepot from a flat rock in the outlying coals of the fire, and filled a tin cup with the hot, black brew. "Since I was a little girl, only ten years old, the don was always very friendly to me. His wife had died years before and he'd never remarried. His children were all grown. He would bring presents down to where I lived in a *jacal* on the don's hacienda."

She rose, strolled around to Longarm's side of the fire, and sank down beside him, pressing her shoulder and hip up against his. She blew on the coffee, sipped, and, staring into the fire and sort of snuggling against Longarm, continued: "Don Cordova once gave me a horse—a fine black mare. He also gave me beautiful, colorful dresses, jewelry, and ribbons for my hair. I didn't think there was anything unusual about all this attention. I enjoyed the mare and the other presents far too much. My father and mother enjoyed them, too, for they were granted certain other privileges not usually granted by dons to their *campesinos*."

Longarm sat with one knee up, elbow resting on the knee, smoking while he listened in silent awe to the girl's story.

"And then one day, three years ago, on my sixteenth birthday, the don invited my parents and me to his sprawling, elegant casa for dinner one evening. It was strange because, aside from his servants, there was only the don there. No one else except for the don, myself, and my parents. It was a wonderful meal—the plates just kept coming from the kitchen, one course after another.

"And then, over a splendid dessert of anise churros with chocolate sauce, the don offered my parents a very handsome sum . . . as well as a proper adobe house on his land . . . for my hand in marriage."

Claudia stared at Longarm as though awaiting his reaction. When he said nothing, but merely stared at her sitting beside him, she said, "Are you with me so far?"

Longarm was imagining what a beautiful creature she had likely been even at sixteen. How nubile and innocent. How enticing to an old pervert. His thoughts must have been reflected in his eyes, because Claudia quirked her mouth corners, nodded grimly, and said, "I see you are."

"So, you married him, I take it . . . ?"

"*Sí.* My mother did not wish to allow it, but my father was enamored of the don's presents and his promise to build them a house, which he did. As for me, I, too, was enamored of the don's presents, and felt that I could not turn down the old goat's offer, though I wanted to in the worst way. But I felt I owed him too much to deny him anything. Not that my wishes would have been respected anyway.

"Two weeks later, the don and I were married in an elaborate ceremony, and that night, on our wedding night, Don Cordova opened his night robe, forced me to my knees before him on the hard stone tiles of his sleeping quarters, and made me suck his cock, and swallow every drop."

Chapter 11

"And if I didn't swallow every drop," Claudia continued with her story, "he would use a braided leather quirt to spank my bare bottom for every drop I did not swallow. Somehow, he claimed to be able to count the drops." She gave a slow, weary sigh. "That first year of our marriage, I went around with a very sore ass—I'll tell you that right now, Longarm!"

"Jesus." Longarm studied for a time on all that Claudia had told him, and then he rolled his cigar around between his lips and said, "So, how did this young Lorca fella come into the picture?"

Claudia sipped her coffee. "The don performed his best sexually when I was young," she said, swallowing. "Over the past couple of years, he has lost his virility. Sometimes it takes quite a bit of manipulating on my part to get him to spend his wretched seed, though I don't mind at all that he no longer spurts very much. But it makes him frustrated. And when he gets frustrated, he gets angry."

"What a sick old bastard," Longarm said, reaching for the coffeepot.

In stunned silence, he refilled Claudia's cup and then his own, and as he set the pot back onto its rock, Claudia said, "When my body filled out and I became a woman, the don's problems seemed to grow. Sadly, however, so too did his desire for me grow. Sometimes he would make me strip very slowly before him, by the crackling hearth in his sleeping quarters. By the time I was completely naked, he would be sobbing like a baby and manipulating his old pecker to try to make it hard.

"Even when I helped with my fingers and mouth, I couldn't get that wizened old worm to get any stiffer than a banana slug. This frustrated the don no end, and the beatings grew worse and worse. Finally, he became so frustrated by my growing beauty and allure, and his own dwindling virility, that he said he couldn't stand to have me around any longer. So he offered to sell me to Señor Lorca and his father, Don Francisco Lorca, for the tidy sum of a half-interest in one of Don Lorca's several gold mines."

"So you were running away when Sandoval caught up to you?"

"*Sí.*" Claudia brushed a fist across her nose. "I lit out the first chance I got. I just threw a few things into some saddlebags—some food and clothes, camping supplies—and I tied a bedroll to the saddle. And I left under cover of darkness. Sandoval and his banditos caught me that morning."

"Where were you heading?"

"To where my parents now live, in the northern foothills of the Sierra Madre. My stepfather and Don Cordova had a falling out, and the don kicked my stepfather and mother and sisters and brothers off the hacienda. My stepfather resettled on his family's land and went back to catching wild horses and breaking them for the local Rurale troupe."

Claudia glanced at Longarm, turning her mouth corners down with chagrin. "It was for them that I took the stolen money. They are such poor people, *mi madre* and *mi papa*. They need it much worse than your government does. I merely wanted to help them to afford a better life. I wanted to take them with me when I fled to Mexico City, where the don wouldn't be so likely to find me and return me to the hacienda . . . or to that weasel, Adriano Lorca!"

Longarm stared at her skeptically over the rim of his coffee cup. "So, you forgave your stepfather for selling you to Don Cordova?"

Claudia sighed and recrossed her long legs at the ankles. "My stepfather was only doing what he thought was best for both me and the rest of the family. True, it was a horror—what I went through at the hands of Don Cordova. But my family didn't know how evil, not to mention unhealthy, he was. Or is." She glanced into the darkness behind them. "Do you think he is still following us? Him and that vile snipe, Adriano Lorca?"

Longarm looked into those wide eyes that appeared inky black in the darkness, the flames of the small fire dancing gold in them. He considered her story for a moment, deciding he had little choice but to believe her. Such a beautiful creature as Claudia Whoever-She-Really-Was could not have been sired by the scrawny, ugly old don whom Longarm had seen in Loco's cantina.

And the wild, half-savage part of her, the unbridled quality that had compelled her to treat him, Longarm, so badly and to take the stolen payroll money for her own, was all Yaqui. He'd tangled with the Mexican natives himself a time or two, and respected how crafty and ferocious they could be.

Señorita Claudia did her blood people right proud. She was no girl to trifle with. He was damned lucky he was still alive. That said, he could understand her plight and felt a vague sadness for her.

"After all you told me," Longarm said, throwing back the last of his coffee and then tossing the dregs into the fire, "I'd say they both have quite a stake in getting you back. Lorca likely bought and paid for you, and the don most likely feels highly insulted. His pride's probably aching like a rotten tooth right now."

She placed a hand on his thigh and squeezed. It was like an electrical charge hitting his groin. Softly, she said, "Will you protect me, Longarm?"

Annoyed by the effect she had on him, he grumbled, "Said I would, didn't I?"

"Will you escort me to my family's little rancho in the foothills of the Sierra Madre? I'm not sure where it is exactly, as I've never been there, so I will need help finding it. And much protection from the depraved sort of hombre who haunts that part of Mexico."

Longarm doffed his hat in frustration, twirled it on his finger. "How far we talkin' about, Claudia? I gotta get this payroll money back to the States."

"Two, maybe three days from here. I know the name of the village the rancho is near. Someone in the village will direct us." Claudia squeezed Longarm's thigh a little harder and pressed her left breast against his side. "I owe you so much already. I will only owe you more." She licked her lips and her dark, gold-flecked, Yaqui eyes crossed slightly with erotic delight. "And after having had to work so hard trying to please the don, I'm sure I can keep you more than satisfied . . . Custis."

She leaned farther over, pressing her breast so hard against his side that he could feel her nipple jutting behind the thin cloth of her dress. She pressed her hand against his already-tight crotch and whispered, "You . . . who needs so little encouragement . . . and knows how to please a girl as well or even better than a girl pleases you . . ."

Her fingers burned through his pants. They felt nearly as hot as a branding iron against his hardening cock.

Longarm narrowed a dubious eye. "Now, Miss Claudia, if I promise to help you find your family, you won't continue to try to lighten my load of all them enticing gringo greenbacks, will you?"

"No." She shook her head seriously. "The money is not mine. I would not disgrace my family with stolen gringo money. I merely lost my head . . . having been poor for so long, and so desperate to get away from the don . . . and knowing how poor my family is." She rose up a little higher on her knees, massaging his cock through his pants. "Please, Longarm, may I please you, as I promised before? To be honest, it is not only you I wish to please. For as long as I've been a woman, I have only been frustrated."

"What about them stable boys you told me about?"

"All lies. The don would not have let me out of his sight long enough for me to fuck a stable boy. The reason

I was such a tigress with you was because, while the don tried to fuck me several times, he could never please me . . . and my blood is hot, Longarm. It is very hot, vibrant Yaqui blood . . . and it calls for a hard cock between my legs now and then! Judge me however you wish, but I need very much to feel like a woman, the way you made me feel the other night, and I have much time to make up for!"

"Oh, Christ," Longarm growled as she used both hands to unbuckle his cartridge belt. He stared down at her hands, keeping a close eye on them, making sure that one didn't sneak over and pull his pistol from its holster.

He glanced at her face. Her foxy smile told him she knew exactly what he was thinking. He was also thinking that he should not be allowing her to put him in such a vulnerable position. But he'd never met anyone quite as alluring and irresistible as the Yaqui siren, Señorita Claudia.

Longarm slid the cartridge belt out from beneath his back, quickly wrapped it around the holster and his Colt .44, and set the rig to his right, in easy reach if he should need it. As he did, Claudia was quickly unbuttoning his fly with her hot, nimble fingers. She reached inside his pants to wrap her hand around his fully erect dong and to gently draw that single-minded snake out of its hole.

Pumping him gently with both hands, she smiled, tossed her hair back behind her head, licked her lips to wet them, and then lowered her mouth over the bulging head of his penis.

He sat back and groaned.

She took turns licking him and sucking him until he thought his heart would explode. She stopped suddenly and stood. She unbuckled her belt, opened her dress, and let it tumble off her shoulders. She was naked beneath it.

She stood grinning down at him, the fire flanking her and bathing one side of her body in flickering crimson. Gold twinkled in her dark eyes.

Longarm stared up at her, his cock throbbing. He kicked out of his boots and trousers. He quickly shed his coat, vest, and shirt, as well. Still standing over him like some dark goddess out of an ancient legend, the red firelight rippling over her magnificent body, she cupped her heavy breasts in her hands and drew each nipple up beneath her chin.

She groaned as she massaged herself, throwing her head back. Then she squatted over Longarm's groin, took his cock in one hand, and impaled herself on the head. Already, she was hot and wet. Her pussy clasped his cock like a resolute hand.

With just the swollen mushroom head inside her, she twisted first one way and then the other and then back again. She moved wildly, her hair flying and obscuring her face, except those eyes with the glowing gold flecks in them.

The wet fur of her snatch raked him delightfully.

Finally, when he'd been teased as much as he could stand, he rolled her onto her back and mounted her. He drove his cock deep inside her. She writhed, opening her knees and groaning and throwing her arms straight out from her shoulders, turning her hands palm down and clawing at the dirt.

He pounded away between her thighs with the regularity of a clock. His sweat-soaked belly slapped against hers. Her breasts rose and fell, jiggling, flattening out against her chest with each thrust of his powerful hips. She mewled and tossed her head and by turns clawed his shoulders and the ground to each side of her.

His passion rose. His blood burned. His seed swelled in his balls.

Finally, he rammed against her and held there, groaning and grinding his molars as he fired his jism deep inside her. She bucked up taut against him, threw her head back, and opened her mouth. Longarm clamped a hand across her lips to muffle her love cries.

He could feel Claudia's warm honey leaking out around his spasming penis. He imagined it sizzling onto the ground beneath them.

While he continued to spend himself, in the corner of his right eye he watched her hand close over his holstered Colt. She managed to unsnap the keeper thong over the hammer and begin to slide the pistol out of its sheath. Longarm chuckled as he ground himself taut against her oozing pussy, and closed his hand over her hand on his gun.

She groaned louder, deep in her chest, and lifted her head and closed her mouth hungrily over his, stabbing his throat with her tongue. Gradually, as her body relaxed, her hand on his gun relaxed, as well, and she looked at the hand and the gun still caught beneath his as though she'd never seen it before.

"I don't know what gets into me sometimes," she said through a weary sigh.

"No." Longarm pulled his dwindling member out of her. "No, I don't know what gets into you, either, Claudia."

He looked at the saddlebags leaning against a near

pine as he sat on his sweaty rump and fixed the keeper thong back over the hammer of his Colt. He looked at the girl, who'd rolled onto her side and drawn her knees toward her belly. Her right breast slumped against her left breast in profile, both slanting toward the ground. They were pale half-moons beneath her arm. Claudia smiled like a girl entering dreamland, and closed her eyes.

Longarm looked at the money-filled saddlebags again.

He shook his head and drew a blanket over Claudia, scowling down at her.

"Gonna be a long ride, ain't it, girl?"

Chapter 12

That same night, something woke Longarm.

He lifted his head from his saddle. Curled against his left side, strands of her hair in his mouth, Claudia groaned softly.

One of the horses gave a soft whicker. Both horses were staring off to Longarm's right, the pearl light of the setting, dime-sized moon in their eyes. In the far distance, a single wolf howled forlornly.

Was it the wolf that had spooked the mounts?

Longarm winced as he gently slid his arm out from beneath Claudia's neck, which she'd used as a pillow. His arm was asleep. It felt like lead. He flexed his hand, wincing, and gained his feet, feeling the hard ground—as well as his violent frolic with Claudia—in every bone and muscle.

"Gettin' too damn old for this," he heard himself mutter in the mountain night's ethereal silence.

He grabbed his rifle and stood naked over Claudia's

curled form, looking around, listening, chicken flesh rising across his body. It was a cool, almost cold night this high in the mountains. The fire was no more than a mound of heaped gray ashes with a single tendril of smoke rising from a small lump of charred wood, peppering the lawman's nostrils.

When Longarm continued to hear only the mournful wails of the wolf, spaced about ten seconds apart, but saw no shadows moving along the perimeters of his camp, he leaned his rifle against the same tree as the loot-filled saddlebags, gathered his strewn clothes, brushed them free of dust and pine needles, and dressed. He donned his hat, wrapped his cartridge belt and Colt around his waist, and grabbed his rifle.

He moved out from the center of the camp, opposite the horses, and stood at the bivouac's southern perimeter. He stared off into the darkness where only a little moonlight penetrated, letting his eyes adjust to the forest's dense shadows. This was the direction in which the horses were staring. If trouble was near, it would likely lie in this direction.

He doubted anyone was within a hundred yards, say. His own ears were keen even while he slept, and he'd come to trust them without reservation. The horses' ears were even keener, and if the bandits who'd harassed Claudia were trying to steal up on the camp, the horses would have let the lawman know with more than a couple of soft whickers.

Possibly, they or someone else was moving around at the perimeter of the horses' hearing . . .

They will come, Claudia had assured him, adding with her beautiful woman's sense of things, *Wouldn't you?*

Longarm sat on a rock and set his rifle across his thighs. He resisted the temptation to smoke a cigar. He had to keep his senses keen, even his sense of smell, and he didn't want to give away his position with the smoke or the glow of a cheroot.

He sat on the rock, motionless, for about twenty minutes. Then he rose, shouldered his rifle, and walked over to where the brook trickled quietly, murmuring like furtive children, in some aspens and cottonwoods at the base of the canyon's southern ridge. He looked around once more, and then set his rifle down on the ground, doffed his hat, leaned out over the bank, and took a long drink of water, slurping it up from the cool, gentle current.

When he lifted his face from the water, he jerked his head up. Something about the night was suddenly different.

He rose to his knees, pricking his ears and casting his gaze in a complete circle around him. Then he realized what was different. The wolf had stopped howling. Beyond the dark camp, the horses were shifting around, more nervous now than when Longarm had first awakened.

The raspy screech of an owl rose suddenly to Longarm's right. It was a harsh, abrasive cry, and it caused his heart to quicken and his shoulders to tighten. He saw the dark shadow of the bird winging off through the tops of the pines maybe fifty feet away, limned briefly by the slanting moonlight before disappearing.

Longarm picked up the Winchester rested across his thighs and caressed the hammer with his thumb. He stared in the direction from which the owl had taken wing. Something or someone had frightened it.

Rising, Longarm began moving slowly in that direction, setting most of his weight on the balls of his boots. He meandered from one dark pine to another as he continued to walk slowly toward the west. The forest floor dropped gradually away beneath him. He followed it down until an outcropping loomed before him—dark and jagged-topped.

He stopped at the edge of the trees and studied the escarpment. Faintly, he picked up the fleeting smell of tobacco smoke. First it was there in the air before him, and then it was gone. He thought he caught another whiff a moment later, but maybe that was only his imagination. The first whiff, however, had not been.

Someone was hunkered down in those rocks, smoking.

The stream was moving faster down this incline than it had been moving near the camp, so it was a little louder here. It prevented Longarm from hearing anything else, much less anyone moving around in the rocks before him. He could see the water faintly—a pearl blur to his left—as it skirted the far left side of the escarpment and continued roiling through its narrow bed on down the canyon.

Longarm slowly, quietly jacked a cartridge into the Winchester's chamber and moved ahead. He reached the escarpment, which appeared about five hundred or so feet high—likely ancient rubble piled here by a glacier—and began following a narrow, pebble-paved path up between the boulders. Around some of the rocks, tough bits of brush grew, silhouetted in the moonlight.

Halfway up the rocks, Longarm stopped. There it was again—the smell of tobacco smoke. It was stronger here. Someone was either perched among these ancient rocks on this side of the escarpment or not far down the other side. Possibly, the outlaws who'd chased Claudia were camped in the canyon near the stream, waiting for the right time to make a play on Longarm for the girl.

Longarm moved even more slowly than before. Now he was glad for the rushing sound of the stream, for it covered any sounds his boots might make on the gravelly path. When he gained the crest of the escarpment, he squatted beside a large boulder and stared into the canyon below and before him.

He was looking for the orange light of a campfire, but there was nothing but darkness down there. From his vantage point, he could make out about fifty yards of clear ground from the base of the escarpment to the trees that filled the canyon. The tops of the pines were silvered by the waning moon. Far to his left, beyond the black hump of the escarpment, lay the silvery stream.

Longarm had just gained his feet when he caught another, much stronger whiff of the tobacco smoke. He dropped back down to a knee as a rifle flashed to his left, maybe thirty feet away. Simultaneous with the rifle's savage belch, the bullet pounded the side of the boulder above and behind Longarm, spraying rock dust and shards.

Longarm twisted around, half-rising, and leveling his Winchester, intending on firing at where he'd seen his assailant's rifle flash. But just then rocks rolled under his right boot heel. That boot slid toward the other one and then he heard himself give a startled yell as he fell on his ass, losing his rifle in a futile attempt to cushion his fall with his hands.

He hit the rocky slope hard, bounced, and then there

was nothing under him except air for what seemed a long time but was probably only two or three seconds before he slammed onto the slope again.

Hard.

"Ugh," he heard himself say.

And then he heard a girl's voice screaming, "Longarm, help me!" just before darkness reached up to wrap its tight, warm fist around him and squeeze consciousness out of every orifice and pore.

Longarm opened his eyes. Soft morning sunlight slanting over the slope sizzled on his retinas, and he squeezed his lids closed. He opened them again only halfway, wincing at the light as well as at the maniacal drumming against the tender back of his head.

His eyes gradually grew accustomed to the light, the texture of which told him it was maybe nine or ten in the morning. But the back of his head continued to grieve him just as severely as it had upon waking. With each beat of his heart, he felt as though a very large savage was rapping a very large sledgehammer against the tender southern end of his skull as hard as he possibly could.

As though the large savage were trying to impress someone even larger.

Longarm gave himself up to the pain and that seemed to help. Slightly. At least, he was able to look up and around and see that he had fallen onto a flat shelf protruding from the slope. Staring straight up about ten feet, he saw the boulder he'd been hunkered against when the shooter had shot at him. Part of the boulder hung precariously over him. The flat shelf he was on was only a little wider than he was.

He rolled onto his right shoulder and stared down to see that if he'd rolled over in his sleep he would have taken another twenty-foot sheer drop onto boulders and scrub brush and then probably rolled down the steep slope all the way to the trees sixty or seventy yards away—a broken and bloody cadaver that would soon have been food for the wildcats and wolves and any grizzly bears that happened to wander by.

Near his boots that were aimed skyward, his rifle bristled from a crack cleaving a boulder in two. Heavily, grinding his jaws against the pain in his skull, he heaved himself to a sitting position. He touched the back of his head. A little, mostly dry blood sprouted from a goose egg back there. Since he wasn't dead yet, this was just another torment that likely wouldn't kill him but just make him miserable and glad to finally get back across the border with . . .

The loot!

He remembered Claudia screaming just before he'd passed out.

"Longarm, help me!"

Longarm found his hat and then pulled his rifle out of the crack in the rock, and dusted it off. He worked the action and inspected the stock to make sure nothing was broken. His heart hammering, filling the large, sledgehammer-wielding savage with youthful vigor, he found a relatively easy way back up the crag to where he'd been shot at. He had little doubt that whoever had shot at him was gone, but he looked around carefully, just to make sure.

Then he stumbled back over the top of the crag and down the other side, recognizing the trail he'd followed last night, though by the light of the rising sun it appeared a glaring misrepresentation of its former, shadow-layered self.

He stumbled up the slope through the trees. Squirrels chittered and birds sang, flitting around the branches. The sun speckled the pine needles and cones, burning off the last of the golden dewdrops. The winey mountain air was tanged with pine resin.

All was well in the forest.

All was well except that when Longarm got back to the camp, the money and the girl were gone. His horse was gone, too, and his gear was strewn around the camp. Someone had obviously kicked his coffeepot, because it had a nice-sized dent in it.

All around the camp were scuff marks of several different pairs of boots. He could see obvious signs of a fight—Claudia's bare footprints showing where she'd made a run for the creek and then swung around to confront her pursuers. The forest duff was churned up here where she'd likely kicked one of her tormenters in the oysters.

Of course, Longarm couldn't be certain she'd done any such thing, but she'd obviously tried to run—probably with the money—and he could see her doing something like that. She'd obviously confronted at least three of the raiders, as three sets of boot prints were entangled with the faint tracks of Claudia's bare feet.

Cursing under his breath, Longarm strode off looking for his horse. Finally, convinced that the men who'd taken Claudia had taken the brindle bay, as well, he tramped back to the camp and looked around like a man inspecting the wreckage of his life remaining in the wake of a cyclone. It didn't help that his head still ached like the blazes.

He stumbled over to the creek, dunked his head, and took a long drink. The cold water made his head hurt worse, but he needed the sustenance.

He doffed his hat and walked back to the wreckage of his camp. He counted the tracks of five men. The five who'd chased Claudia on the other side of the flooded arroyo. The five Longarm hadn't shot.

The five he now wished like hell he'd gunned down like cans in a row.

"Damn fool," he said, castigating himself.

He doffed his hat and fingered the goose egg at the back of his head. He sighed and returned his hat to his head.

A rifle barked. The bullet blew his hat off.

Chapter 13

Longarm had leaned his rifle against a near tree. Now he started to lunge for it, but stopped when the rifle crashed twice more, blowing up pine needles and dirt two feet in front of him.

A man's Spanish-accented voice said, "I suggest you stay right where you are, gringo lawman. Toss away your *pistola* and raise your hands to your shoulders, or I will drill you through your lying heart!"

Reluctantly, Longarm tossed his Colt away. He raised his hands and stared off toward the creek just as the old don stepped out from behind a pine between Longarm and the gurgling stream. Longarm glimpsed more movement in the periphery of his vision. When he glanced to his right and his left, he saw several more men, all in the brightly colored clothing of vaqueros—albeit well-armed vaqueros—step out from behind trees or boulders. One was Adriano, the Fancy Dan whom Claudia had been promised . . . or sold . . . to.

Adriano Lorca had stepped out from behind the tree to the don's right. He aimed a shiny Winchester straight out from his right hip, and his dark eyes blazed from beneath the brim of his palm leaf sombrero. The don walked toward Longarm, holding his own Winchester, which a lanyard attached to his shoulder, straight out from his right side. The spurs of his high-topped, fancily stitched black boots rang like chimes.

As he strode toward the lawman, he stretched his thin lips back from his teeth and annunciated very clearly and loudly, "Where is my daughter, gringo lawman? And why did you not only insult me but waste my time by sending me off in the wrong direction? Hurry! I want a straight answer or I will blow your heart out and leave you to the mountains!"

Longarm said, "How did you know . . . ?"

"I got that disgusting creature Loco to tell me everything. You are down here illegally, hunting for stolen American money. Maybe you were also hunting for beautiful Mexican señoritas, as well!"

Before Longarm could retort, the old man stopped ten feet away from him and said, "Hurry! Out with it! Where is she? If you've murdered her, I'll—!"

Adriano Lorca lurched forward, jabbing his rifle toward Longarm's belly. "I'll get it out of him! One bullet to the gringo lawman's guts, and then one in each knee, and—"

"You won't get one thing out of me but blood, Chico! And a whole lot of cursin'." Longarm glared at the young Mexican who stood not three feet away from him. "Now, back off, Chico, and aim that rifle in another direction or

I'll take it away from you, shove it up your ass, and trigger it!"

"How dare you speak to me that way!"

Adriano drove the rifle forward. Before it could ram into Longarm's belly, the lawman stepped sideways, jerked the gun out of the kid's grasp, and, holding it by its forestock, backhanded him. Adriano screamed and stumbled backward before getting a spur caught on the ground and falling to his ass.

"*Bastardo!*" Adriano grated through clenched teeth, holding one black-gloved hand to his red cheek. To the don, he snarled, "Keel him! Keel him now!"

The other vaqueros shifted around uneasily, murmuring.

The don had been all business. But he seemed slightly amused by the sight of his future son-in-law's unceremonious declawing. There was a sparkle in his eye as he glanced from Adriano to Longarm, but he dipped his chin at the kid's rifle in Longarm's hand and said, "Drop that one now, too, señor."

Longarm flung the rifle with disgust into the brush. "Your . . . uh . . . *daughter's* gone, Cordova. A mixed bunch of outlaws came into camp last night and took her. From here, they headed south."

Through narrowed, foxy eyes, the don scrutinized the camp—the strewn gear and the torn-up ground. He looked at Longarm. "Where were you?"

"Someone ambushed me in them rocks yonder. Woke up just a few minutes ago with a powerful headache."

Don Cordova stared off. Longarm thought he saw a genuine worry in the old man's muddy brown eyes. "South, you say? Who? How many? If they've harmed her . . . !"

"You mean, before you could?" Longarm snarled at the man. "Or until you got your interest in the Lorca family gold mines?"

The old man snapped a flabbergasted look at him. *"Qué?"*

"But she's not even really your daughter, is she? No, she's your slave. Your love slave!"

Cordova staggered up to Longarm, scowling up into the taller man's face. "*Love* slave? Why, I'll have you whipped for such an—!"

Longarm grabbed the barrel of the rifle the old man was aiming at him and jerked the don into his arms, turning him so that his back was pressed against Longarm's chest. Almost instantly, Longarm had drawn his .44-caliber over-and-under pocket pistol from his right vest pocket, and now he had the little popper cocked and pressed against Don Cordova's liver-spotted right temple. He'd dropped the man's rifle. He turn the old man slightly so all his men could see the suddenly compromised position their patrón was in.

Cordova cursed him in Spanish. Ignoring the tongue-lashing, Longarm glared at the men around him, including young Lorca, who was still on the ground, pressing his hand to the red welt on his cheek.

"Anyone shoots me, your employer'll be joinin' me on that long ride. And you'll be out of a job quicker'n you can say pass the *bacanora*!"

The seven vaqueros were crouched around him, eyes wide, fingers drawn taut against the triggers of their carbines.

"Do not shoot!" the don raked out, still gritting his teeth. He struggled against Longarm, but he was no match for the taller, younger, more powerful man. "Don't shoot, you idiots!"

"Not only don't shoot," Longarm said, "but release the hammers on those rifles and toss 'em to the ground. Then your pistol belts." He pressed the cocked derringer harder against the old man's temple until Cordova yelped from the pain. "*Vamonos!* Tell 'em, Don!"

"Sí, vamonos! Vamonos!"

By ones and twos, the seven vaqueros released their rifles' cocked hammers with soft clicks. They tossed the weapons to the ground. Glaring at Longarm and muttering under their breaths as well as cutting conspiratorial looks at one another, they unbuckled their gun belts.

Longarm spied movement to his right. He jerked his head toward young Lorca. He jerked the derringer toward him then, too, and the pistol gave a hollow pop as it leaped in Longarm's hand. Flames lashed toward Lorca, and the young man yowled as his big Russian revolver went careening out of his hand to land with a plop behind him.

Lorca yowled again, clutching his right hand with his left. Blood dribbled down from a graze across the top of the kid's gun hand.

"You damn fool," Longarm spat out.

He was in no mood for more foolishness. The stolen money he'd risked life and limb, not to mention his job, to ride down here for was steadily making its way farther and farther away from him. That was his top priority, but he couldn't deny that he was more than a little worried about Claudia, as well, though he knew the girl was rather adept at taking care of herself.

Don Cordova laid into the young fool, Lorca, with a loud, rasping string of Spanish while Longarm returned the gun to the don's temple. "Anyone else tries anything like that," the lawman said, "you'll be carrying the don home across his horse, and you'll all be ridin' the grub line."

Two of the vaqueros were still holding their pistol belts. Now they dropped them and stepped back, turning their mouth corners down beneath their drooping mustaches.

Longarm ordered the men back farther away from their guns. Then he walked the don over to where he'd thrown his Colt, picked it up, and exchanged the derringer for it in his right hand. He clicked the Colt's hammer back, and pressed the barrel of the larger revolver against the don's head.

"You," he said, nodding to the shortest and youngest of the vaqueros standing across the fire from him and the don. "You run back to wherever you stowed your horses and ride one back here to me. Better make it quick. If you're gone for more than five minutes, I'm gonna shoot your boss and all your friends. That's a lot of blood on your soul, amigo. You make sure that when you return, you don't have any weapons in your hands. *Comprendes?*"

The young man, who wore a billowy green neckerchief that matched his dusty green, steeple-crowned sombrero, looked at the don. Cordova nodded. The young vaquero turned and went running down the slope through the pines, deerskin breeches slapping his thighs.

"Don, you be a good *hacendado* now, and go sit over there on the ground next to your future son-in-law, though it don't look to me like there's gonna be any weddin', if your daughter has anything to say about it, and I hear she does." Longarm couldn't help grinning at that last, as he gave the old man a shove toward young Lorca. Turning to the seven others, who were regarding him like he was a wounded grizzly who'd just wandered into their bunkhouse, he said, "You fellas have a seat, too. Relax. As soon as that horse gets here, I'll be movin' on."

"Where do you think you are going, gringo lawman?" the old don said as he eased his slender, brittle-looking body onto a rock beside young Lorca, who continued to cradle his bloody hand against his chest and give Longarm the stink-eye.

"I'm goin' after them owlhoots that got your daughter."

"Why? For my daughter?" Don Cordova gestured with his hand to the young man with the bloody hand sitting to his right. "She has chosen Señor Lorca, and he has chosen her. They are due to be married in three days!"

"Not the way your so-called *daughter* tells it." Longarm gave a caustic chuff as he holstered his Colt and retrieved his Winchester from where he'd leaned it against the tree. "And, anyways, I don't care so much about her as the owlhoots. They got somethin' I want."

"Ah, yes," the don said, nodding his understanding. "They must have taken the money you came down here to retrieve as well as my daughter, huh? It appears to me, amigo, that we have somewhat similar interests in the same gang of men."

"Shut up, Don. I've had enough out of you. You ain't goin' nowhere with me, and as for Claudia, you can forget her. If I find her alive, I won't be sendin' her back to you but on to her *real* folks down south, in the Sierra Madre."

"Her *real* folks?" both the don and Adriano Lorca said at the same time, looking at Longarm as though at a bull they'd just now realized had grown an extra head.

The don alone said, "What are you saying, crazy gringo? What is this about her *real* folks . . . *where?* . . . in the *Sierra Madre?*" He tapped his chest with both hands, leaning forward for emphasis. "I, Don Cordova, am her real folks. Claudia's dear mother died two years ago, but I am still alive, and I am her father despite what . . ."

The don let his voice trail off. His eyes widened as he stared at Longarm, a realization coming to him, and then he lifted his chin toward the treetops as he slapped his thigh and roared with laughter.

"She told you she was raised by Yaqui, didn't she?"

More laughter, thigh slapping, and head wagging.

And then, so suddenly as to be odd, Don Cordova turned as sober as a judge at a street hanging. "And you believed her."

He looked disappointed in Longarm, who fought off the urge to feel chagrined. He narrowed a skeptical eye. "You mean, she ain't no Yaqui?"

The don shook his head sadly.

"You didn't give her Yaqui family a casa on the Cordova hacienda and then marry her, and . . ." Longarm flushed under the realization that he'd been played for a sucker. He wasn't about to start detailing all the bedroom high jinks the girl had reported—the stuff about drinking every bit of the don's vile spend lest he whip her for each drop that she spilled. And now, going through it all quickly in his mind, he realized how crazy it all sounded.

"Yaqui?" young Lorca said, shifting his incredulous gaze between Longarm and the don. "Casa on the hacienda . . . ?"

"My daughter has long since been both blessed and

plagued with an overactive imagination, though unfortunately it was mostly her family who felt plagued by Claudia's colorful conjurings. The fact of the matter is, sir, my daughter is . . . well . . ." Cordova twirled a finger near his right ear, ". . . a little . . . well . . . *disorganized* in her thinking. She doesn't always think clearly. Often her fanciful imagination gets in the way of such clarity.

"Since Claudia was a small child, she fancied herself a Yaqui princess after she saw some Yaqui vaqueros working cattle on the hacienda. She was amazed by the dark little men and their dark little half-savage children, who lived in brush huts along the river bottoms. And she instantly deemed herself one of those self-sufficient, earthy people. I think the attraction for her was in seeing how wild and free they were. At least wild and free was how she saw them. Maybe even their dangerousness, their savageness attracted her. My wife was deathly afraid of them, though my father and myself had long ago made peace with the local band of Yaqui.

"Of course, Claudia herself was brought up quite formally, quite *civilly*—I'm sure you can understand. In her later years, she would often drift back to such fanciful thinking, imagining and even *attesting* that she was one of them. Especially when she felt herself under a mental strain. And I am sorry that you have to hear this under such circumstances, young Adriano, but I am afraid that the prospect of the wedding has been a bit of a strain on our dear Claudia."

"Strain?" said the young man. "But . . . but she has professed her love to me many times! She assured me in her last letter, before I arrived at Hacienda de la Cordova, that she couldn't wait to marry me!"

"I'm sure that's all true, Adriano," the don said. "Claudia is just a little confused. I'm sure when we have her home, she'll see how mercurial and impractical she has been.

"Speaking of that," Cordova added, turning to Longarm, anxiety darkening his gaze, "We are only wasting time. We must get after that gang that has my daughter. I saw them on the trail ahead of us, and if they are who I think they are, they are very dangerous men, indeed! And they will soon be meeting up with many more!"

Chapter 14

The seven horses thundered down a trail slanting into a wide, deep ravine. Claudia, hands tied to her saddle horn, was on her own horse leg by the last male rider in the pack. The reins of Longarm's brindle bay were tied to the tail of the señorita's Arab, bringing up the rear. The gang of sweating, unshaven men—two gringos, two Mexicans, and a big half-breed with a greasy red bandanna—reined up on the canyon floor where a narrow desert stream ran along the base of a striated sandstone wall.

The gang was out of the piney mountains now, deadheading south, and the sun was a blacksmith's forge. The sandstone ridge, however, offered shade as well as cool springwater gurgling over a bed of cracked granite and limestone.

As the man leading Claudia's Arab came to a halt behind the others, who were quickly dismounting by the water, he leaped down from his saddle, walked back to the stallion, and slid a a bowie knife from a belt sheath.

His pale blue eyes raked Claudia up and down as he cut her free of the ropes tying her hands to the saddle horn. He grinned as he stared at the well-filled corset of her dress, and then grabbed her arm and jerked her out of her saddle.

Claudia gave a yelp as she tumbled down the horse's right stirrup fender and landed, fortunately, in a patch of relatively soft sand that formed a delta of sorts along the stream. She sat up, shaking her hair from her eyes, and cursed the man—a wiry gringo in nondescript, sweat-stained, dusty trail garb—with whom she'd been riding. The gringo laughed as he sheathed the knife and inspected the girl sitting on the ground with her bare legs spread.

"Damn, but you're a fine piece of ass!" He turned toward where the other four men had clumped together, the gang leader, a gringo called Ballenger, opening the flap on one of the saddlebag pouches. "Hey, Ballenger, ain't she a fine piece of ass?"

"Yeah, she's a fine piece of *chiquita*, all right," Ballenger said, glancing up from the saddlebags. "And she comes with a nice load of greenbacks, too."

They hadn't taken the time the previous night, when they'd kidnapped Claudia out of Longarm's camp, to closely inspect the money they'd also taken from the bivouac. All they'd known was that as well as a beautiful señorita they'd happened upon a pair of saddlebags bulging with American money. They'd confiscated both and, apparently thinking they had other men on their trail, booted their horses south through the mountains, keeping up a dangerous, breakneck pace all night long.

The man nearest Claudia glowered down at her. He was practically salivating. She thought she could see a bulge in his crotch. He appeared torn between her and the money, however. The girl gave a sigh of relief when he finally turned away and walked over to where the others were kneeling by the stream, pulling the wads of greenbacks out of the bags.

Claudia watched them for a time, cursing her luck. First Sandoval, then Longarm, now these *pendejos*, balling up her plans. Somehow, she had to figure a way out of her current situation. Preferrably, with the money.

Somehow.

It didn't look good.

Men . . .

She rose to her feet and was turning toward the stream when one of the men said, "Uh-uh-uh—you stay right where you are, señorita!"

It was the leader, Ballenger, who wore a black hat to match his black goatee and black eyes, though he appeared to be all white man. He wore three pistols, two on his hips, another, smaller revolver hanging from a cord around his neck.

"Do you mind if I get a drink of water?" Claudia asked, all sass.

Ballenger grinned knowingly at her, raking his eyes down her legs to her bare feet. They hadn't let her put on her boots, for fear she'd run away. Barefoot, she was less likely to get any wild ideas about fleeing.

"You can get all the water you want. Just don't get any ideas about runnin'. We fellas got other ideas fer you!" Ballenger winked at her.

The others glanced away from the money to ogle her and whoop and yell like rabid coyotes.

Claudia rolled her eyes and then stepped between the

horses, all of which had their heads lowered over the water, and dropped to her knees in the shallow stream. While the men yammered delightedly about the money—*her* money—she lowered her face to the stream, bathing her face and drinking.

Lifting her face from the soothing water, she swept her hair straight back over the top of her head with her arm and looked around. The horses stood in the water ahead and to her right, switching their tails and drinking. The men were gathered just past them, near where the spring curved around behind them. A few boulders and willows lined the stream beyond the men, offering shade.

Claudia figured the men were about thirty feet away from her. She looked at all seven horses lined up in the stream. More specifically, she looked at the rifles jutting from leather sheaths all strapped to the saddles on the horses' right sides.

Claudia's heart quickened. She jerked another look at the men, most of whom either had their backs to her or were kneeling sideways to her, all five ooing and awing over the money.

The girl's heart beat faster.

Could she reach one of those rifles before one of the men could draw his revolver and shoot her? She had nothing to lose. Why not make a try?

She glanced once more at the men. Ballenger was rifling through the packets, making a hasty count. The others were fondling the packets that Ballenger tossed onto the ground after counting them. None of the men was watching Claudia.

She rose slowly from her knees to her feet. Chewing her bottom lip, she moved just as slowly forward, setting one bare foot and then the other into the stream. The cool water felt good. Soothing. She took another step forward. Still, the men were yammering about the money as they counted, unable to believe their unexpected good fortune.

Claudia looked at the horse nearest her, a buckskin. The rifle jutted up from the right side, angled forward and away from her. Claudia took another slow step and then another, and then she was on the horse's right side.

Chewing her lip until it almost bled, she glanced once more at the men. Still, they were not looking at her. She looked at the walnut stock of the rifle. The brass butt plate cast a flickering reflection on the water. Claudia reached up and forward, closed her hand over the stock, took another step forward, and began pulling the rifle out of the sheath, wincing as it made a soft *snick* sound, sliding against the leather.

She gave a grunt as she continued sliding the rifle up out of the leather, and her heart hammered as the barrel came free. The rifle was heavier than she'd expected. As she closed one hand around the forestock and the other around the rifle's neck and began to lower the cocking mechanism, to seat a cartridge in the chamber, a gun roared three times so quickly that all three roars seemed one prolonged cacophony.

Water plumed in front of Claudia, splashing her. She fell back against the horse from which she'd taken the rifle just as the horse whinnied and sidled away from the gun reports. The others horses all jerked with starts, lifting their heads and curling their tails, and Claudia fell into the stream with a scream, dropping the rifle, which splashed into the stream beside her.

She rose to a sitting position, the water covering her,

the rifle glistening at the bottom of the stream to her left, and peeled the strands of her wet hair away from her eyes. All five bandits were standing and staring at her. Ballenger was aiming his gun at her, smoke curling from the barrel.

His eyes were sharp. The saddlebags and packets of greenbacks were strewn at his feet. A couple of the men held more packets in their hands.

The big half-breed wearing the red bandanna said to Ballenger, "She needs to be taught a lesson, Dean."

"Yeah, Dean," said the man she'd been riding with. "That girl needs a lesson, and I'm just the one to teach her."

The two Mexicans grinned. One swabbed his sweating forehead with a grimy sleeve.

The man Claudia had been riding with stepped toward her, unbuttoning the fly of his faded, smoke-stained trousers.

Ballenger nudged him aside with his smoking pistol and, keeping his eyes on Claudia, said, "She's mine, fellas. All mine. You keep your grubby hands off of her."

The big half-breed opened his mouth to object, but Ballenger cut him off with "Shut up, Crow."

The big half-breed's face crumpled in an indignant scowl. The others also looked miffed as Ballenger stepped forward, coming at Claudia like a bull in a ring. He paused to lean his rifle against a rock, and then he said, "You boys can watch if you want. See how a real man fucks."

He looked so dark and menacing that Claudia's heart turned a double somersault. Every limb tingled. Involuntarily, she screamed, scrambled to her feet, and ran straight up the stream along the base of the red ridge wall, further frightening the horses that splashed out of her way. She ran only several yards before Ballenger was on her, tripping her.

Claudia fell into the water, and then the outlaw leader pulled her up by a handful of her hair at the base of her neck, and half-dragged, half-led her to the bank, where the sand was relatively soft. He threw her down hard and she rolled over, glaring up at him, water streaming down her face.

"Bastard!" she screeched. "Pig! Leave me alone! I am the daughter of Don Cordova, and if you . . . !"

"Shut up!" Ballenger snarled, standing between her spread legs. His dark shadow angled over her.

The other men wandered up to within about ten feet behind him, now no longer looking as much disappointed that they couldn't have her first as they were eager to watch the show. Scowling down at her, his eyes large and black in their deep sockets mantled by black brows, Ballenger finished opening his fly. He pulled out his cock, which was standing up, straight and red and swollen.

Claudia, always the survivor, widened her eyes, feigning admiration. She whistled under her breath and said, "Whoa, amigo. You're one hell of an hombre!"

"*Muy* impressive, eh, bitch?" Ballenger said, dropping to his knees between her spread legs and wagging his manhood at her. "You know a nice rod when you see one, huh?"

"*Sí, sí,*" Claudia said in feigned awe, staring at the man's jutting cock as he leaned toward her. "*Sí, sí*—I know a nice rod when I see one."

"You treat me right, señorita," Ballenger said, grinning and winking at her as he used both hands to rip her dress wide open, baring her breasts, "I'll treat you right. Meanin', if I like what you give me, I maybe won't cut your throat after I fuck you."

He lowered his eyes to her breasts, and he whistled. "Look at you!"

"Enough looking," Claudia said, glancing at the two pistols jutting from the holsters on his hips. He'd tossed the one that he'd had hanging around his neck to the ground. But he still wore the two. The pig didn't appear to be in any hurry to shed them . . . even for romance.

Claudia inwardly smiled at that, glancing at the jutting walnut grips once more.

"Enough looking, *muy* hombre," she said, reaching forward and stroking his cock with both her hands, causing his eyelids to drop half over his black eyes. "Now it's time to put this handsome organ where all your bluster is, huh? What do you think, Ballenger—do you really think you can please a woman like me? Let me warn you, this is not my first time."

"No," Ballenger laughed, "I was startin' to get the idea it wasn't, señorita." His eyes rolled back as she continued to stroke him. "But you better get prepared for the best fuck of your entire life!"

He'd just dropped down on top of her and had pressed the head of his swollen member against her snatch, when she reached down and grabbed both pistols from their holsters. He had his eyes closed but when she clicked the hammers back, he opened them.

He opened his mouth also, to scream, but if he got any of that scream out, it was drowned by the twin roars of his own pistols.

Chapter 15

Claudia had planted the barrels of both pistols against the underside of Ballenger's chin and squeezed the triggers at the same time. Warm blood splashed over her as the bullets tore through the man's mouth and exited the back of his head, near the top.

He collapsed on top of her, and she sort of rolled his quivering corpse to one side.

The other outlaws stood clawing at their revolvers, but they were so deep in shock at what had just happened that all four appeared as though they'd never drawn and fired a six-shooter before in their lives. They hopped around, yelling, clawing at their holsters.

Claudia had taken regular target practice at the hacienda—her father had thought it necessary for her to know how to shoot in the event of a Yaqui or Apache attack—so she had little trouble quickly lining up her sites on the man she'd ridden with and drilling a .44 round through the dead center of his chest.

When she'd sent him stumbling back, howling, she gained her knees and quickly dispatched both Mexicans. That left Crow, who by this time had drawn his own two revolvers and stood crouched amid the other dead and dying men around him. The big half-breed with the savage, pockmarked face stood glaring at Claudia over the barrel of his right-hand gun.

His long, sweat-damp, dusty hair blew around his massive head in the dry breeze. The horses had splashed a ways down the stream and stood staring warily back toward the source of all the commotion as well as the fresh blood scents.

Claudia knelt with her own two pistols cocked. Her dress hung off her left shoulder, leaving her naked. Her breasts and face were red from the gallon or so of Ballenger's blood that had washed over her. It dribbled down her forehead and cheeks and dripped slowly off her left nipple and onto her contracting and expanding belly.

She stared at Crow. He stared back at her.

The half-breed's eyes flicked across her naked body and then returned to her eyes. Claudia smiled delightedly.

"What we got here, Crow," she said slowly, raspily, "is a Mexican standoff."

"Uh-huh," Crow said. "But I'm not Mex. I'm Sioux from up in Dakota. Half-Sioux, half-Irish."

"That sounds like fun," Claudia said.

"Wouldn't you like to know?"

"Can't say as I wouldn't." Claudia glanced at the money strewn around the rocks and ground behind the big man in black denims and calico shirt and wearing a string of bear claws around his massive neck. "I got a proposition for you, Crow. Can we ease these gun hammers down and discuss it?"

"What's to discuss?" Crow kept his guns aimed at Claudia. "You just killed my amigos. You'll kill me if I lower these pistols. You're a devil woman, that's who you are."

Claudia smiled larger, with unabashed delight. "*Sí.* I do have a good bit of El Diablo in me. That being said, I have my pride, and when I say you can trust me, you can bet the seed bull you can trust me, amigo. I come from a good family. I wasn't raised by wolves, like your friends there."

"What about me?" Crow asked, his turn to smile. "I was raised by wolves. A whole pack of 'em, señorita."

"Yeah, well, that's what I like about you. You're the man who can help me get where I need to be. And you're just the kind of man who can enjoy the gifts I have to offer you for helping get me there."

"Oh, yeah? Enjoy those gifts like Ballenger did?"

"No guns allowed. Just you and me, though I hope you'll understand if I feel the need to clean myself up a little first."

Crow stared at her and blinked. He looked at her askance and then he said, "On three."

Claudia blinked slowly.

"One," Crow said. "Two . . . three. . . ."

All four hammers eased down against the firing pins with barely audible clicks.

Claudia and Crow did not lower their pistols, however, until Crow, grinning, and showing a chipped front tooth, counted to three again. Then they lowered their pistols, albeit cautiously, tensely, watching each other closely.

Claudia gained her feet, giving the big savage a good

look at her body. Confident he would not, could not shoot her now—in fact, he seemed to feast on her with those dark, animal eyes—she chuckled through her teeth, tossed the pistols to the ground, and walked out into the stream.

She sat down in the shallow water, on her ass, and stretched her legs out in front of her, letting her feet loll in the slow-moving current. Slowly, she splashed water over her breasts, rubbing and cupping them and washing away the blood. She washed it gently from her arms and shoulders and her face. While she did, Crow stood at the edge of the stream, watching her hungrily.

"Well?" Claudia said. "What're you waiting for?"

She splashed him with her foot. The big man jerked to life. He'd shucked out of his clothes—all except his necklace of bear claws—and came splashing out into the stream, cock jutting.

Claudia laughed and lay back in the stream, spreading her legs for him.

Longarm kicked the dead man onto his back. He grimaced at the bloody ruin of the cadaver's head. The man's penis was hanging out of his open fly. It looked like a pale worm one might find under a log, its head dangling over the man's denim-clad right thigh.

"*Christo!*" said Don Cordova, sitting his sleek dun Arabian behind Longarm. "What in the name of God happened . . . ?"

The old don let his voice trail off. Longarm looked up at him and the pack of vaqueros, including Adriano Lorca, sitting their dusty, sweat-silvered Arabians behind him. Lorca was riding double with one of the vaqueros. It had made sense for young Lorca to double up, since the hand that Longarm had grazed with a .44 slug was grieving him, making holding the reins difficult for the prissy lad.

Longarm had agreed to ride with Don Cordova and the old man's vaqueros after the don had explained that the pack of outlaws who'd taken Claudia, not to mention the stolen army payroll money, was part of a much larger pack. The part of the pack that had Claudia and the American greenbacks would likely meet up with the rest of the gang somewhere soon in the southern mountains.

If and when that happened, they would likely number at least a dozen seasoned desperadoes. Longarm would be wise to not try to take them on alone. Without the don's help, the gringo lawman would likely never see the army payroll money again, and his desperate ride south of the border would have been in vain.

Not to mention fatal.

What had finally convinced Longarm to throw in with the don was the fact that the old man was being trailed by a wagon from his hacienda. That old, heavy-wheeled buckboard was clattering on down the slanting ridge trail now, a brass-canistered Gatling gun jostling and reflecting javelins of bright sunlight from the wagon's creaky bed.

The wagon itself was driven by an old, one-eyed, bearded, stove-up vaquero named Milandro Alvarez. Apparently, the don had purchased the Gatling gun from the Mexican government when a band of unheeled, raggedy-assed *revolucionarios* had been threatening to overrun his hacienda several years ago. The Gatling gun was an old Civil War model, but the don assured Longarm that it was still in perfect firing condition and that old Milandro Alvarez knew how to fire it most expertly.

When the don had assured Longarm that Alvarez had blown many a revolution-minded peon into eternity, old Alvarez had spread a grin brown with tobacco juice running down both sides of his wrinkled up old mouth.

Now, as the wagon clattered to a stop a ways off to the side of the horseback riders, old Alvarez set the break with a grunt, looked around, made a face, shook his head, and crossed himself.

"Holy shit, huh?" he said, sliding his rheumy brown eyes between Longarm and the don.

"*Sí,*" Don Cordova said, nodding gravely at the dead men's remains. "Holy shit."

"What do you suppose happened?" Longarm asked the don.

He didn't wait for an answer. The question had been rhetorical. He had what he considered a fairly sound idea about what had occurred here, one corroborated by the fact that the dead man nearest him had his dick hanging out.

Which meant that said dead man—who fit Don Cordova's earlier description of a gringo outlaw leader named Dean Ballenger—had been in the process of using his exposed dick, or at least *attempting* to use it, when his brains had been blown out the back of his skull.

Not that Ballenger hadn't been force-fed his just desserts.

Pondering the situation, brows knitted, Longarm tossed his reins up to young Adriano Lorca, shucked his rifle from the young man's saddle sheath, and then walked downstream toward where what he assumed to be the dead men's horses were grazing the galetta grass growing among rocks and willows lining the water. When he'd managed to run his brindle bay down, he slid his rifle into the empty sheath, and led the animal back along the stream.

As he walked past a willow blocking his view of the Mexicans, all of whom had now dismounted and were leading their thirsty horses into the stream, he saw the don and young Lorca standing closely together, facing each other, arguing.

Their Spanish was too fast for Longarm to get a solid grip on, but that they were arguing about Claudia there was little doubt in the lawman's mind. The argument ended when the don slapped the slightly taller Lorca twice—once with his open palm, once with the back of his hand—and then wheeled and walked away.

Lorca stumbled backward, stunned and fuming, nostrils flaring. When he saw Longarm staring at him, he snarled a curse and then waded out into the stream before kneeling to remove the bandanna he'd wrapped around his hand and soak it.

Longarm tied the reins of the bay to a willow by the stream. He glanced once more at the dead man lying with his pale pecker drooping and then walked over to where the don sat on a rock, pensively filling a porcelain-bowled pipe.

Longarm dug a cheroot out of the pocket of his frock coat, struck a lucifer to life on his thumbnail, and regarded the don severely. "Out with it."

When the don's face turned red with fury and he turned his dark, hateful eyes on Longarm, the lawman said, "You might be able to beat a deep path around the old schoolyard privy with that silly young Lorca fella, but you fool around with me, Don Cordova, you're gonna piss-burn me. You're daughter's already done that. Multiple times. Not to mention pulled the wool over my eyes more times than I'd like to admit to you or anyone else.

"Now I want to know what in the hell that lovely little polecat is up to and where she's headed. Obviously, she killed those men back there. Maybe her and one of the others she might have turned against his own gang. Whatever happened here, she was likely an instigator, and she and the fifth rider obviously rode off together. I got a feelin' you know where they're headed and likely why they're headed there, and it's time to tell me."

The don laughed with too much vehemence for the lack of humor in his eyes. "Or you'll do what, Longarm? You're a long ways from home. You have no jurisdiction down here. In fact, you have no *right* to be down here!"

Longarm's cheeks burned. He glanced at the vaqueros, several of whom were eyeing him dubiously, hands near their holstered pistol butts. Longarm turned back to the don. The man was right. He was all bluster down here south of the border. He'd been burned severely by a beautiful, devilish woman, and he had no one to blame but himself.

He was damned frustrated, but there was nothing he could do to make Don Cordova tell him what the old man knew about Claudia's wicked motives and intentions. All he could do was keep following her until he caught up with the stolen money.

If he ever would . . .

He wheeled and walked several yards into the rocks, staring off down the canyon bristling with cacti of every shape and size and shade of green. Beyond the canyon, the desert rolled off toward the purple humps of the Sierra Madre in the far, misty distance.

The lawman was so distracted that he didn't hear anyone walk up behind him until someone closed a hand over his shoulder. He turned to see Don Cordova staring gravely up at him from the shade cast by his broad sombrero brim.

Chapter 16

"I understand your frustration, Longarm," the don said. He sighed, turned to stand beside the tall lawman, and stared off down the canyon. "I, too, am deeply frustrated. As, I assure you, have been most men who have fallen under my lovely daughter's spell."

Longarm drew on the cigar and watched the don, waiting. He had a feeling an answer to his question was forthcoming, and he was right. The don puffed his pipe pensively, with a troubled air, and then he said, still staring off down the sun-burnished canyon toward the purple humps of the Sierra Madre, "As I said before, my daughter has an overactive imagination. But that wasn't the entire story."

The don puffed the pipe for another thoughtful minute or so. Then he knocked the dottle from the bowl onto the gravel, ground the gray ashes with his boot heel, and said, "My daughter has had a troubled life. She has been headstrong for as long as I can remember, and very hard to control since she became old enough to walk. Even harder when she filled out and became the beautiful woman she is now. But let me shorten the story for you, Longarm. The horses will have their wind back soon, and we must ride hard to catch up to her."

"All right—the short version," Longarm said, watching the man eagerly while taking another long drag off his cigar.

"The man whom she said kidnapped her off the hacienda—Sandoval. He was, in fact, her half brother. And may Madre Maria forgive me for saying this, though it is sadly the truth, Sandoval was also her lover."

Longarm arched a brow. He hadn't thought that anything more could ever surprise him about Claudia Cordova, or rock him almost literally back on his heels. He'd been wrong.

"*Half-brother* and *lover?*"

"*Sí*, it is true." The old don sniffed. For a moment, Longarm thought the he was going to cry, but then he continued with: "I kicked Sandoval off the hacienda long ago, when he was only fourteen. He was even more headstrong—and mean and nasty—than his sister. He, like his great-grandfather on his mother's side, was a born outlaw devil straight out of the bowels of hell.

"Nothing made that boy happier than to walk all over authority, and to do the exact opposite from what he'd been told by his elders who were only trying to raise him properly. But . . . back to making my story short . . . Sandoval began running with another desperado, a man by the name of Jesus Fortuna. Fortuna was raising hell on my hacienda for years, and then I was informed by some of my closest men that Claudia had been seen with Fortuna."

Longarm didn't have to ask what "seen" meant. He knew the girl well enough to know just how she'd most likely been "seen" with Jesus Fortuna.

"Sandoval and Fortuna had been closely aligned. They were bandits, cattle rustlers, gold and silver thieves, even slave traders. But now I believe that Claudia has aligned herself solely with Fortuna, and that a storm may have been brewing between the two men— between their two factions. My daughter was in the middle, manipulating both men for her own devious desires . . . which included getting very rich and living high on the hog in Mexico City."

"What about them dead men over there?" Longarm said, gesturing with his cigar. "They have anything to do with Sandoval and Fortuna?"

"As far as I know, their gang had nothing to do with Sandoval and Fortuna." The don smiled balefully. "Those men were merely more not-so-innocent bystanders caught in my daughter's intricately woven web. Why she left one of them alive, I have no idea. Maybe to help her through these dangerous mountains, haunted by more men just like those she killed, as she travels to meet up with Fortuna somewhere in the Sierra Madre. I believe she loves, or at least thinks she loves, Fortuna, and intends to share her newfound wealth with him and only him."

"The stolen army money."

"*Sí.* That is about the size of it. I apologize, señor."

"What about young Lorca?"

"I arranged for them to be married. They had been close once, as children. I thought moving Claudia off my hacienda and onto Don Lorca's, as his son's wife, would spare her from her own devious ways. I guess I lied to myself when I thought she was growing out of those ways.

I thought her marrying young Lorca would complete her transition."

The old don gave a long, weary sigh, blowing his wizened cheeks out. "How wrong I was!"

"What do you intend to do when you catch up to her?" Longarm asked him.

The don lifted his eyes to Longarm's and quirked a miserable smile. "I will do to her what I do to rabid dogs and coyotes on the hacienda. I will put her, once and for all, out of her misery. As well as my own. She is not only dangerous to herself, but to others."

The don flared his nostrils, angry, determined. "She must be shot down. I will bring her home tied over her horse and bury her beside her mother at Hacienda de Cordova. And that will be the end of my dear Claudia. I will forbid her name to be spoken ever again!"

The don adjusted his hat, turned on a heel, and trudged back to where the others were resting and smoking near the horses.

Scowling skeptically, Longarm watched him go.

Claudia reined her fine Arab stallion up at the crest of a barren hill, shook her hair back away from her eyes, and stared down the other side. A smile stretched slowly across the señorita's rich mouth.

A broad canyon opened before her—pale as flour but stippled with willows that sheathed a little stream running along the base of the canyon's south side, to Claudia's right. Some irrigated patches of corn and wheat grew along the stream, flanked by the brush *jacals* of the *campesinos* who worked the fields.

Up the long, steep, rocky slope on Claudia's left, a

large, brown adobe church stood, a grim sentinel over the canyon. About two hundred yards down the slope from the church, between the church and the stream, sprawled a village of pale adobes and rickety wooden stock pens. Now in the midday heat, nothing much moved among the glaring white or dun-colored structures except an occasional drift of dust lifted by some animal being herded between stock pens.

From Claudia's vantage point, the village might have been abandoned. But all of Mexico appeared abandoned in the middle of a hot, desert-summer day. This was the time of siesta. Soon would come the tightening of the violin strings and the tuning of the mandolins for the rollicking fiesta ahead, which would start after the villagers' bellies had been filled with supper and the sun had gone down.

The village stretched unevenly across the slope. On the village's other side, on the shoulder of a rise that formed a rib of sorts on the side of the ridge, running perpendicular to the canyon floor and the stream, lay an ancient, sprawling, Moorish-style casa, the red tiles of its roof glaring in the midday sun.

Claudia stared at the casa. Slowly, the smile already quirking her lips grew wider. Absently, she reached back to stroke the saddlebags bulging with the American greenbacks. As she did, the clomps of hooves rose, and Crow rode up and reined in beside her.

"You keep up a hell of a pace for a *chiquita*," he grumbled. The big half-breed stared down at the canyon. "Poco Carmen?"

"Sí."

"This is where you meet Fortuna, eh?"

"Sí."

"Well, I tell you what, sister," the big man said. "I reckon we part ways here. I don't want nothin' to do with that crazy bean-eater, Fortuna. Okay, I got you here. I fulfilled my part of the bargain. We sure had fun, you an' me, but I'll be takin' my reward and headin' back north."

Crow held out his large hand, palm up.

He grinned lustily at her. "I sure would like to give you another poke, but I reckon a packet of that American money will do me." He gave his head a hard, fateful wag. "A piece of ass like you don't come along every month for the likes of ole Crow—that's for sure."

He frowned as his eyes dropped, and he saw the revolver she was aiming at him from her right hip.

"Hey, just hold on now! I fulfilled my part—"

Claudia's Colt belched.

The slug punched a hole in the big man's broad chest, at the place where his open calico shirt came down and formed a V over his breastbone, about three inches beneath the lowest dip of his bear claw necklace. He grunted, jerked, dropped his chin to stare down at the frothy blood bubbling out of the hole.

"Hey, you," he said, clawing at the hole with both hands, as though it were merely a speck of dust he could wipe away. He looked at her with an expression of both perplexity and sadness in his mud black eyes. "We . . . we had a deal, dammit!"

He sagged back away from Claudia. He flailed his hands at his saddle horn, but while his fingers raked the horn, they did not wrap themselves around it. Crow dropped down the far side of his horse and hit the ground with a heavy thump. Pale dust blew up around his mount, which whinnied, buck-kicked, and trotted a ways off the trail, glancing back accusingly at Claudia.

"Sorry, horse," the señorita called to the mount. "I have no beef with you. Only Crow. You see, I don't like sharing my hard-earned money!"

Laughing, she holstered the Colt and then booted the Arab on down the hill and into the canyon.

As she followed the bending trail into the village, several villagers, sleeping beneath their sombreros under brush arbors along both sides of the shit- and straw-flecked street, poked their sombreros up far enough to peek out from beneath the brims. Their eyes widened. They poked their hats up onto their foreheads and sat up straight to get a good look at the lovely *chiquita* galloping the fine, cream Arab into their town, her thick chestnut hair jouncing and dancing, tits jostling around inside her low-cut dress like two good-sized piglets in a gunnysack.

A vision, to be sure! A sight for sore eyes!

The villagers—there were four men and one boy in ragged pajamas who was not so young that he couldn't appreciate a well-turned female—all looked at one another as though making sure they weren't dreaming. One man whistled. Another spread a toothless grin. A third glanced at the boy and jerked his chin in the direction in which the *chiquita* had disappeared.

The boy nodded and went running up the street into the girl's sifting dust. His father looked at a fellow villager sitting on the other side of the street, grinned, and cupped a hand to his crotch.

Claudia galloped the Arab on through the village, scaring chickens and hazing a couple of bleating goats into alleys, and reined up in front of the sprawling casa on the village's far side. The sprawling house with its arched windows and doors and several wooden balconies, sat on a shelf against the hill behind it, surrounded by barrel cactus and sycamores fed by underground springs.

A tattered flag of Mexico snapped atop a sun-silvered pole in front of the place, which had once been the home of a wealthy don who had owned the entire canyon. The don had been gunned down by Fortuna himself, when the don came home to find that Fortuna's gang had invaded the place and Fortuna himself was in bed with the don's wife and daughter.

Since then, Fortuna had taken over control of the canyon and the village, and his name was spoken around this part of Chihuahua in hushed and fearful tones, fingers pressed to quivering lips. The casa was now one of the most notorious saloons and brothels in all of southern Chihuahua, and home to Fortuna's thirty-man band of soulless cutthroats.

Claudia swung down from the Arab's back, tied the reins at the wrought-iron hitching post, and hefted the bulging saddlebags over her shoulder. Adjusting the Colt in its holster on her right hip, she padded barefoot up the hot stone steps, crossed the open, flagstone-paved gallery, and passed through the casa's broad open doorway.

Behind her, the little brown boy in ragged peon's pajamas hunched furtively behind a barrel cactus just up the slope from the main trail, staring.

Chapter 17

Claudia stopped just inside what had once been the casa's broad, high-ceilinged main entrance hall. These days it was a cool, dark saloon with an ornate bar shipped in from God's knows where running along the right-hand wall.

At the rear of the long, deep room, a broad stone staircase with a scrolled wooden rail climbed into the dark heights of the second story, which was a balcony ringing the saloon on three sides. Close doors shone darkly up there, behind an ornately carved balustrade.

The saloon itself was a stinking ruin. Claudia wrinkled her nose against the stench of piss, vomit, sweat, sex, and sour liquor. Stale tobacco smoke hung in the air over the room, though as Claudia's eyes adjusted to the shadows, she could see only four or five men in the drinking hall. Two of the five were asleep—one on the floor against a large stone pillar, another with his head down on one of the twenty or so dilapidated wooden tables. Two more were playing a desultory game of cards halfway down the room.

Another—a tall, lean man in an unadorned, low-crowned black sombrero and long, deerskin duster—stood at the bar, staring over his shoulder at the lovely newcomer. One silver hoop dangled from his left ear. A sawed-off, double-barreled shotgun hung from a lanyard down his back.

He blinked once, slowly, and then raised a shot glass to his lips. "*Chiquita,*" Hector Santiago said, blinking his queer blue eyes again, stretching his bold, black mustache in a welcoming smile. "Welcome, welcome. What brings you out here to this canker on El Diablo's ass?" He threw the last of the shot back and then set the glass down loudly on the bar and beckoned the short, swarthy bartender over for a refill.

To Claudia, Santiago said, "You come back for me? Ah, that's sweet." He glanced through the doorless opening behind her. "Where is your notorious half brother?"

"Sandoval is dead, Hector."

Hector winced, but there was no real sadness in it. "Isn't that the way it goes, though, señorita?"

"Where is Jesus?"

Ignoring the question, Santiago muttered something to the bartender, who then filled a second shot glass with the same clear liquid as that in Santiago's glass. Santiago lifted both shot glasses up in front of his face, and then he walked too carefully over to a table, and said, "Come. Drink with me."

"I asked you where Jesus was," Claudia said sharply.

"Forget about him. He forgets about you. He is upstairs in his room, doing God knows what to which one of his pretty *putas*. I am the better man, *Chiquita*. The two of us together—we could rule the world. And have a hell of a fine time doing it." He raked Claudia's breasts with his eyes, blinked slowly, and jerked his chin back slightly. "Come on—have a drink with your old friend Hector. I have always admired you, *Chiquita*."

Claudia strode over and stood on the other side of the tall, blue-eyed Mexican's table. "You have always admired my tits," she said, taking the shot glass from him.

She raised the glass in salute and threw back the mescal. It burned going down, but it eased the aches and pains and the heat of the sun in her flesh, the chafes and scrapes on her bare feet.

She slammed the glass down on the table. "Where is he?"

"What you got there, Claudia?" Santiago was looking at the saddlebags draped across her right shoulder.

Claudia walked around the table and stopped beside Santiago. She drew her Colt from its holster, clicked the hammer back, and pressed the barrel against the underside of the man's chin.

"Wouldn't you like to know."

Santiago had to keep his head straight, because of the pistol, but he slanted a sneering look down past the gun to the lovely señorita holding it.

"He's upstairs, huh—Jesus?" Claudia quirked a smile, depressed the Colt's hammer. "Be seeing you, Santiago. Enjoy the mescal."

She returned the revolver to its holster and walked on down the bar, glancing once at the swarthy bartender staring at her dubiously while twisting an upswept end of his mustache, and mounted the stairs. She walked along the balcony and into a dimly lit hallway in which several cracked or broken statues stood like ghosts in the shadows. Her bare feet slapped the cool stone tiles.

She followed the hall to the room she knew to be Fortuna's. Her father had always kept a close eye on her back at the hacienda, but when he suspected she'd been getting into trouble against his best efforts to keep his thumb on her, he'd shipped her off to the nuns at San Vincente.

Such incarcerations, as she saw them, had happened many times over the course of her twenty years. However, most times the convent at San Vincente hadn't been able to hold the likes of the devious, promiscuous young Claudia. The nuns had been enough afraid of the demon-like, bewitching beauty to have not reported such escapades to her father . . . escapades which had included rendezvous with her half brother, Sandoval, and his cohort, Jesus Fortuna.

Claudia had always wanted wealth and independence as well as high adventure—a means to vent the violent, surreal energy and desires pent up inside her. Her father's wealth, however, was far from hers. The old man kept tight rein on the Cordova purse strings. But now, with the stolen army payroll cash, she had enough money to become fully independent of the old don and to live life entirely on her own terms.

It was, however, a man's world. Which meant she needed at least one man to help her survive, to share her adventures, and—last but not least—to satisfy her womanly desires until someone else better hung and more easily commanded came along.

Claudia lifted her hand to knock on the heavy wooden door before her but stayed the movement when she heard a girl groan on the other side of the door. She lowered her hand to the latch and lifted it. The door loosened in its frame. Claudia pushed the door open a few inches and peered through the crack.

A large, four-poster bed abutted the opposite wall, sticking out into Jesus Fortuna's massive personal living and sleeping quarters. Fortuna lay naked on the bed— though Claudia could not tell if the man was really Fortuna. But she thought it was from the familiar grunts and groans.

She couldn't see the man's face or much of him at all above his waist, because a girl with long, black hair was straddling him, the girl's slender, brown back facing Claudia, who stood at the room's entrance. The girl was bouncing very slowly up and down on her knees, raising and lowering her pussy over Fortuna's cock, which Claudia could see when the dusky-skinned *puta* raised her round, brown ass and just before she lowered it ever so slowly again, sliding her pussy back down to the outlaw leader's hips.

Claudia chewed her lip as she stepped into the room. Very slowly, holding her breath, she closed the door behind her, lifting the latch so it did not click. Crouching so that the man beneath the *puta* would not see her, she moved slowly toward the foot of the bed.

She closed her upper front teeth over her bottom lip, deviously, as she slid her Colt from its holster. Holding the gun straight out in front of her, she reached over the foot of the bed and placed the gun barrel against the small, dark, puckered hole of the *puta*'s ass.

"*Gna-ahhhh!*" the whore cried, jerking forward and dropping to her forearms.

The man she was fucking looked over her slender left

shoulder. Jesus Fortuna gave a startled, bellowing scream and yelled, "*Claudia! Mi amor!*"

The whore tried to wriggle away from Claudia's Colt, which she now cocked loudly and rammed even harder against the *puta*'s asshole. "Are you having a good time, you cheating bastard, Jesus?" she yelled. "Having a real good time with the *putas*?"

"Claudia, *por favor*!" he yelled as the whore buried her face in his shoulder. He glanced down to see the pistol and gave another startled yell as he raised his hands to his ears, palms facing Claudia. "*Dios mío*, crazy woman. What in the hell do you think you're doing?"

"I think I'm going to pop a pill through this whore's asshole, you cheating *pendejo*!" Claudia screamed, gritting her teeth. "Give me one good reason why I shouldn't kill you both with one shot and save me the price of a bullet! One good reason, you cheating bastard, Jesus!"

The *puta* screamed and shivered and wagged her ass.

"Claudia!" Jesus shouted, his mustache-mantled mouth forming a perfect O as he stared in horror at the young woman threatening both him and the whore in such a miserably personal way. "*Por favor*—I beg your forgiveness. I lost my head. I am *sorry*, *Chiquita*, but it's been a while since we've been together, and you know how we men are. We have to have our sap bled off now and then or we go insane!"

"What will you do to make it up to me, Jesus?"

Fortuna blinked up at Claudia, dubious. "Wha . . . Huh? What . . . whatever you want, my beautiful *Chiquita*! Just name it!"

Claudia let a smile spread slowly across her rich lips. "Marry me?"

Fortuna blinked again, this time in disbelief. He stared up at Claudia as though he wasn't quite sure what she'd said. Even the whore turned her head to look up at the crazy woman ramming the Colt's barrel against her asshole, skepticism narrowing her Indian-dark eyes.

"I will ask it only once more, *mi amor*," Claudia said. "Will you marry me?"

Fortuna obviously didn't know if she was serious. His jaw hung toward his chest for another ten seconds, in shock and terror. And then he said, "Yes, sure! Sure, sure—I will marry you, *Chiquita*. Whatever you want! Just . . . now . . . would you please uncock the revolver and kindly aim it in another direction?"

He gave a tense smile.

It was almost dark when Longarm topped the rise that looked down on Poco Carmen. The blue smoke of cook fires hung over the pale little village sprawled across the rocky shoulder of the mountain. The soft strains of a single violin made their way through the purple gloaming and up the hill to Longarm's ears.

His ears just then picked up the rustle of brush off the trail's right side. Instantly, his double-action Colt was in his hand. He rolled a half-smoked, unlit cheroot from one side of his mouth to the other as he put the brindle bay off the trail and into the brush.

An angry mewling sounded. More brush thrashed and crunched under several sets of paws, and then he saw the outlines of the two *lobos* trotting down the slope away from him, one's eyes showing yellow as it cast an angry glance back over its shoulder.

Longarm was sitting his bay, staring down at what the

lobos had been chewing on, when Don Cordova and his men rode up the hill behind him and then rode off the trail to gather around him, their horses snorting and tossing their heads, weary from the long ride, thirsty and hungry.

"What is it?" the don asked the lawman.

Longarm canted his head at the bulky dead man lying belly-down in the brush, where the *lobos* had dragged him and torn open the seat of his trousers in an attempt to access the most succulent organs.

"*Madre de Dios!*" the don said, crossing himself. Several of the vaqueros did the same.

Adriano Lorca just sat staring grimly down from his Arab's back. He hadn't said anything since the don had explained to him, during the afternoon ride, all the nasty little and not-so-little truths about his daughter. Lorca seemed to have been taken completely by surprise by all of it. He continued riding along with the don's pack, but Longarm had no idea of the young man's intentions.

Surely young Lorca wasn't so taken with the girl's succulent figure that he still intended to marry her . . . ?

"Your daughter leaves quite a trail of bread crumbs," Longarm said.

"*Sí*," the don said quietly, staring down at the dead man, the fresh blood glistening in the last light. "She does at that."

Distantly, Longarm could hear the rattling of the wagon carrying the Gatling gun.

"You fellas stay here," he told the don as he turned to stare down at the village, more and more lamps and torches winking to life as the night settled over the canyon.

"What do you mean—'stay here'?" Cordova was incredulous. "My daughter is down there."

"Yeah, well, so's the stolen money I've ridden all this way to fetch. I don't want anything or anyone fucking that up. I'm done bone tired of all that. If we all ride down there like a pack of the *lobos* that were just tearing into this dead hombre's ass, that's exactly what will happen."

Longarm shook his head and fished a lucifer out of his shirt pocket. "One man ridin' in alone will look a whole lot less suspicious." He raked the match across his holster and touched the sputtering flame to the end of his half-smoked cigar. "I'll ride in and fetch both the money and your daughter. The money for me, your daughter for you. I reckon you deserve to have her back, though I'd just as soon not be around when you drill a bullet through her head . . . even though she sure as hell deserves it."

Puffing smoke, Longarm turned his brindle bay back onto the trail. As he started down the hill, he glanced over his shoulder to say, "Park that wagon in the brush at the top of the hill there. And for god's sake have it loaded and ready to go in case later, when I leave that village—and I intend to leave well before sunup tomorrow—I have some uninvited *compañeros!*"

Chapter 18

Longarm let the brindle bay have its head, and the weary cavalry remount slowed to a slow walk as it entered the little Mexican village of Poco Carmen. Longarm had rested the mount less than an hour ago, and had let it eat plenty of grass and drink all the water it had wanted at a run-out spring, but he could feel the fatigue deep in the horse's muscles beneath the saddle.

Or was it Longarm's own weariness he was feeling deep in his own bones, and he was merely attributing it to the horse? Whatever the case, he hoped the stalwart beast still had some corn in its bin, so to speak. He doubted there would be much rest for either of them this night. The faster he got his hands back on the army loot, and got himself and the horse headed back to the border, the better.

As for Claudia—he didn't care what happened to her. It was only the money he cared about now.

Or so he told himself . . .

As the horse clomped slowly along the trace paved here and there with ancient crushed brick, Longarm shuttled his gaze from one side of the street to the other. A couple of cantinas were already doing a brisk business, judging by the number of men pushing through their doors in twos and threes. The vaqueros were coming in from the haciendas and tying their frisky mounts to hitching posts.

Occasionally, a woman's throaty laugh rose from one of the unmarked adobe hovels flanked by small, sun-silvered, brush-roofed galleries. Those cantinas with two or more stories were likely parlor houses, though Longarm doubted they boasted much in the way of parlors. Likely just cribs a little larger than jail cells and outfitted with beds hardly bigger than cots.

The lawman wasn't sure how he was going to go about locating his quarry . . . and money . . . until he came to a handful of peons bunched in the street outside one of these two-story affairs. On the second-floor balcony of the place, two painted ladies in bright, skimpy dresses were conversing in coquettish tones with a couple of the peons, all of whom were staggering drunk. The peons were standing by a small fire they'd built in the street, near a sprawling cottonwood and across from a dry stone fountain. They were passing a heavy stone jug among themselves.

Longarm knew that, being a gringo, he'd look out of place this deep in Mexico, but he had a feeling this neck of Chihuahua probably saw all types passing through—mostly outlaw types—so he probably wouldn't stand out all that much, after all. Besides, with his sun-leathered skin and dark hair and mustache, he could pass for at least part-Mexican, and his badge wasn't pinned anywhere on his person but residing in his wallet.

He reined up beside one of the peons, leaned down to tap the man on his shoulder, and asked the hombre in passable Spanish if he'd seen a pretty señorita ride through the village in the past several hours. The man's eyes lit up, reflecting the dancing flames of oil pots and torches. But as he turned to size up the big man in the black frock coat sitting the tall, weary-eyed bay, he acquired a suspicious look.

Longarm reached into his pants pocket and tossed the peon a five-dollar gold piece. As the stoop-shouldered, bearded peon stared at the coin in his palm, as though he weren't quite sure what to make of it, Longarm said, "A night's worth of tequila on the gringo. Which way'd she head, old-timer?"

Realizing the valuable chunk of metal he was holding in his hand, the man looked up at Longarm again, and again his eyes danced jubilantly. "*Sí, sí.* I saw her, señor. But I know not where . . ." He let his voice trail off and then lifted his chin to stare over the bay's ass at something or someone on the other side of the street.

"Giuseppe!" the old peon called.

Presently, a little boy in ragged peon's pajamas, oversized serape, and tattered sombrero came dashing from an alley mouth. He held two empty bottles in the crook of one arm, and Longarm figured the kid was running mescal and tequila from the cantinas to the cribs residing in dangerous back alleys.

The bearded, stoop-shouldered peon spoke to the boy, Giuseppe, much too quickly for Longarm to follow beyond two or three words, but the kid's sudden, toothy grin was universal. He'd seen the girl, all right, and knew exactly where she'd headed.

Staring up at Longarm, the kid turned shrewd businessman as he hiked one shoulder, arched a brow, and raised one small, brown hand, palm up. Longarm chuckled and dropped a five-dollar gold piece into the boy's hand. The boy stared at the coin as though it were the most sacred of all talismans, and then dropped the bottles at his feet and said in near perfect English, "This way, señor. I show you!"

With that, he ran up the street, sandals slapping his heels.

Longarm booted the brindle bay ahead, following the running lad. The street twisted around but generally trailed east between rows of ancient adobes, some lit and showing occupation, some as dark as graves. Occasionally, figures moved in the darkness—men and women together, murmuring. There were the infrequent strains of mandolins, sudden, muffled laughter, and even a couple of gunshots.

But otherwise the eastern end of the little village was dark and quiet—at least, until Longarm followed the running Giuseppe around another bend and an enormous structure came into view, perched on a northern slope a little ways above the town. The casa, or whatever it was, was lit up like a Mexican Christmas tree. Man-shaped shadows jostled against the lights of windows, torches, and oil pots.

The sporadic pops of pistol fire had kicked up, as well, and now Longarm saw that the shooters were somewhere outside the sprawling casa. Following Giuseppe up a curving two-track trail between deep ravines, Longarm automatically reached forward and loosened his Winchester in its saddle boot.

The boy stopped about fifty yards from the casa, beckoning Longarm. When the lawman drew abreast of the kid, Giuseppe pointed to the sprawling, red-tiled adobe that boasted a long, broad front gallery and a second-story balcony equally as long and wide. Probably a house owned by a wealthy landowner at one time, the casa now appeared to be the scene of a rather larger fandango.

The shooting, however, as well as the faint whiffs of sweet perfume, opium, and marijuana that Longarm picked up on the quiet breeze, bespoke an outlaw den. One that was most likely every bit as savage and dangerous as a nest of angry diamondbacks.

Longarm found himself not at all surprised that Claudia would have headed for such a place. This is where she'd met up with Fortuna.

Now, how in the hell was Longarm going to finagle the girl and the loot out of such a place without becoming just another story about a gringo lawman who'd vanished down Mexico way?

"Thanks, kid," Longarm said, swinging down from the saddle. "I think."

He gave Giuseppe the bay's reins. He also gave him another gold coin. "Tie him to that hitchrack I saw in front of that pink adobe back the way we came, will you? I'll pick him up there."

The boy was breathless over the second gold coin in his palm. *"Muchas gracias, señor!"* With that, he went running back down the sloping trail to the main road, the bay trotting along behind him.

Longarm had left his Winchester in its boot. He

couldn't very well walk into this lair that teemed with desperadoes loaded for bear. That would attract more attention that he himself would. His Colt and his derringer would have to do.

"God help me," he whispered, feeling the nerves leaping around in his back at each pop of the pistols the men were firing off the casa's southern side.

As he strode past the shooters, continuing toward the casa's broad front gallery, he saw that about six men—they were little more than silhouettes fringed in salmon torchlight—were placing bets and shooting at cans and bottles. Laughing and yelling and having a real good time. A little farther on, another man was fucking a girl bent forward over a rain barrel, her frilly, salmon-green dress on the ground around the girl's brown ankles.

The girl was groaning and sighing and the man was giving hard, savage grunts as he thrust his bare hips against her ass.

There were a good twenty horses tied to the multiple hitchracks fronting the casa. Longarm stepped between two horses and mounted the gallery. The shadows of men jostled around him—murmuring, smoking, laughing. He could smell tequila and mescal, and the cloying odors of opium and marijuana were stronger. And every time a pistol belched at the end of the casa, his trigger finger twitched.

He went on inside and was surprised that there weren't that many men in the main drinking hall—at least, not as many as he'd figured there would be. He was glad to see that there were outlaws of every stripe and color, including several obvious gringos and two black men. He didn't stand out much at all.

Feeling slightly relieved, he hooked his thumbs behind his cartridge belt and walked over to the bar, where he ordered a bottle of tequila from a short, stocky gent with long, coal-black hair gathered in a braid and a grisly mess of a pockmarked face. The barman didn't seem unduly surprised that Longarm paid in American coinage. He merely shrugged and dropped the coin into a bucket on the floor behind him.

The lawman took his bottle and glass over to a table near the bar and slacked into a chair. He wasn't all that surprised not to see Claudia in the main drinking hall. She'd ridden hard all day, and she was likely still taking a siesta or generally relaxing, possibly eating, in one of the sprawling casa's many rooms. If she had been here, he would have slouched around in the room's many shadows and bided his time until he could get her alone and find out where she'd stowed his money.

Then he'd have gone to work getting both her and the money out of here in any way that presented himself.

There were several girls working the room. One had caught Longarm's eye, and she his, though she was otherwise occupied, sitting on the knee of one of the several men watching and betting on an arm wrestling match going on at a table near the rear of the room. Longarm winked at her, for just then an idea had occurred to him, and he sat back in his chair and began slowly sipping his tequila, biding his time.

He was in a hurry to get the hell out of Poco Carmen, to be sure, but he couldn't act on that urge. He had to relax as much as he could, take his time, wait to locate the right entrance to the rooms above and around him, in one of which was the girl and the money he'd come for.

Just then a fellow gringo came up to his table and stood over him, scowling down at him. The man canted his head to one side, brushed a gloved hand across his nose, and said, "Mister, where in the hell have I seen you before? I'll be hanged if you don't look familiar as old sin!"

Chapter 19

Longarm pretended to scrutinize the tall, lean hombre staring down at him. The man was maybe forty, and the lid hung lazily down over his left, pale green eye, giving him a halfway sleepy look. Halfway because the other eye was wide open. Cow-stupid, but wide open. The man also had a three-inch scar running across the brow mantling his lazy-lidded eye.

Right away, Longarm recognized Lazy Lid as Cooper Stanley. The federal lawman had run across the horse thief and murderer some years ago, in a roadhouse near Julesburg, Colorado. Cooper had been a wanted man then as he was now, but he hadn't been wanted near as much as the three other men Longarm had been after, so he'd let Stanley go.

Now he wished he hadn't.

"Sorry, pard," Longarm said, grinning affably up at the man but ready to kill him here and now if he needed to.

"But I can't help you out at all. Not at all. Why, I wouldn't know you from Adam's off ox. Don't that beat all?"

That didn't seem to appease Cooper Stanley one bit. He merely canted his head the other way and scowled down at Longarm, fingering the fringe of beard on his chin.

Just as he opened his mouth to retort, a girl's voice said, "Chico, you old reprobate—look what the cat dragged in!" The whore whom Longarm had been playing eye patty-cake with earlier dropped into his lap and wrapped her arms around his neck. "Where have you been, Chico, and what has kept you away from your dear Esmeralda for wayyy too long?"

"Well, howdy, Esmeralda!" Longarm said, not sure what the hell was going on, but playing along just the same. "I'll be a monkey's uncle if you ain't a sight for these sore old eyes!"

"When are you going to make an honest woman of me, Chico?"

"Well, now, I, uh . . ."

"Oh, shut up, you big fool!" Esmeralda touched her nose to his and pulled on his mustaches. "Why don't you just take me upstairs and ram your hard one between my legs? I need to start earning my keep around here or Jesus will throw me out!"

Longarm laughed, glancing at the tall gringo scowling down at him, apparently still trying to remember where he'd seen him before. "When Stanley's memory stretched back through his alcohol haze," a quiet but menacing voice was whispering into Longarm's left ear, "all hell was going to break loose."

"That sounds as fine as frog hair to this old saddle tramp, Esmeralda. Yessir, fine as frog hair!"

Esmeralda crawled down off his lap. Longarm rose and grabbed his bottle and shot glass. He purposely did not look at Cooper again as he wrapped his free right arm around Esmeralda's shoulders and she wrapped her right arm around his waist. They strolled along the bar, heading for the broad, stone stairs at the rear of the room.

"Where've you been keeping yourself, big man?" Esmeralda said.

"Me?" Longarm said. "Oh, hell . . ."

They continued with the made-up chitchat as they climbed the stairs and she led him off down a hallway littered with cigarette butts, empty bottles, and both male and female underclothing of every stripe. They passed a statue of a Spanish conquistador outfitted in a pink corset and lacy black bustier, a ragged-tipped cheroot protruding from a crack between its stone lips.

When Esmeralda had led him through a heavy door and into a room in which a single candle guttered from a dented bean can, she closed the door and pressed her back to it, gazing up at him, her expression suddenly serious.

"You owe me big, Marshal Long."

Longarm gaped at her. He hemmed and hawed before saying, "I'm afraid you have me at a slight disadvantage."

"I am Miguel Fuentes's daughter, Pilar."

Longarm glowered at her, trying to place the names she'd just rattled off. "Fuentes? Why, he's a—"

"He *was* a deputy United States marshal stationed in Tucson. Until he was killed by Jesus Fortuna. Bushwhacked while taking me, his only daughter, to church one Sunday morning. Fortuna's gang had just robbed the bank, and they grabbed me after killing my father. That was two years ago. I have been down here ever since. Whoring for Fortuna and the pigs in his gang."

"Holy shit," Longarm muttered, staring down at her, the memory fog clearing.

He'd worked with Fuentes in Arizona several times. Once or twice, he'd supped at Fuentes's tiny casa on the outskirts of Tucson. He had a vague memory of a pretty, black-eyed little girl—the only female in his house, Fuentes's wife having died giving birth to their only child—silently serving the meal and then clearing the table afterward. She'd given him a couple of foxy smiles but had otherwise kept her eyes bashfully averted.

"Yeah . . . yeah, I remember. I'd heard that Miguel was killed. I was up in Dakota at the time, didn't learn about it till months later. I do believe everyone thought you were dead, Pilar!"

"Yes, well, that was a convenient assumption, since Fortuna hauled me across the border and all the way down here to this hellhole."

Pilar Fuentes pressed her hands against his chest and stared up at him with a beseeching look. "Please, Longarm—whatever you are down here for, you must promise to take me with you when you leave." She sobbed. "Please! I have waited for sooo long to be rescued!"

She pressed a hand against his groin. He felt her warm, pliant fingers through his trousers. "I will make it worth your time! Down here, I have learned to ply the trade rather well."

Longarm for once didn't enjoy the tug of lust in his crotch. "That won't be necessary, Pilar," he said, his mind racing, not quite able to catch up to the fact that his responsibilities had suddenly doubled. "I'll get you out of here. Maybe, at the same time, you can help me out with what brought me here in the first place."

"Anything!"

"You likely saw the pretty señorita who rode in here earlier."

"I did not see her, but I heard from the other girls about her. Fortuna's woman. I hear she comes from a rich family." There was bitterness in the girl's voice.

"You know where she is?"

Pilar shrugged. "With Fortuna, I would assume."

"Where?"

She shrugged again. "His room."

"You know where that is?"

"Sí."

Longarm's heartbeat quickened. Finding Fortuna's room, and thus Claudia, had been the first order of business on his docket.

He looked down at Pilar. She was attired in a simple but elaborately embroidered Mexican dress that left her shoulders and most of her legs bare. Her feet were bare, as well. Nubbin breasts poked out behind the skimpy frock.

"Best throw somethin' a little more comfortable for riding on," Longarm told her. "Then you can show me to Fortuna's room."

"Sí, sí!" The girl sobbed in delight as she quickly began moving about the small, cluttered room.

Less than three minutes later, she'd shed the dress and exchanged it for canvas pajama bottoms, a simple calico blouse, a straw hat, and rope sandals. She filled a bladder flask from a pitcher of water and slung the deerskin lanyard around her neck.

"I have been waiting for this moment for a long time," she said. "Come. I will show you to Fortuna's room."

She opened the door and glanced into the hall. When she gave him the all-clear sign, Longarm followed her out into the hall, drawing her door quietly closed behind him. She beckoned to him, and one hand wrapped over the grips of his holstered .44, he followed her down one hall and then another. Twice, they had to step into a recessed doorway to let one of the whores and a customer pass on to the way to the whore's room.

Finally, when they'd seemingly been walking in circles through the massive ruin of the ancient casa, they stopped at a heavy, scrolled oak door. Pilar meaningfully rolled her eyes at the elaborate panel.

"Wait here," Longarm said, gently moving her to one side and sliding his Colt from its holster.

From behind the door, moaning sounded. Both a man's and a woman's. The door didn't appear to have a lock on it, though it could have been barred from the inside.

Only one way to find out.

He gingerly tripped the latch.

The moaning grew louder as the door swung slowly open. Longarm doffed his hat, tossed it back into the hall, and slid his right eye around the side of the door. He blinked as though to clear his vision. But, no, his eye wasn't deceiving him. There were three people in the room. Two on the bed. One standing to the left of the bed.

The two on the bed were women. Naked women. Claudia and a brown-skinned girl. Claudia lay on her back, bent legs spread. The girl crouched between her spread knees, hands massaging Claudia's thighs while she licked Claudia's pussy. Claudia was half-turned onto one shoulder, her head to the side. A tall, rail-thin man with long, dark brown hair, a scraggly mustache and beard, and protruding ribs, was thrusting his cock in and out of Claudia's mouth. He had his fists on his hips, head thrown back, eyes squeezed shut.

He gritted his teeth, groaning with each thrust of his impossibly skinny hips.

Longarm inadvertently nudged the door. It opened wider, a hinge squawking. The man thrusting his cock in and out of Claudia's open mouth, who could only have been Jesus Fortuna, whipped his head toward the door, wide eyes bright with shock.

Longarm shouldered the door wide open. "Hold it, Fortuna!"

But the skinny, naked man was already reaching for a revolver jutting from a holster hanging on a near bedpost.

Claudia pulled her head back off of Fortuna's cock, turned toward Longarm, and screamed. At the same time, the girl who'd been eating Claudia's pussy also turned her head and screamed. A half second later, as Fortuna twisted around, leveling a long-barreled, silver-chased Remington at Longarm, the lawman aimed and triggered his Colt once, twice, three times.

The first bullet plowed through Fortuna's left shoulder. The next one hit him low in the chest. As he was falling back, screaming, Longarm had aimed a little more carefully, and sent the third round punching through Fortuna's forehead, an inch above his left eye.

Fortuna bounced off the wall flanking the bed and dropped like a fifty-pound feed sack to the floor.

Claudia had only screamed once, but the other girl was holding a hand in front of her open mouth through which she was hurling one ear-rattling scream after another.

"Shut the hell up!" Longarm snarled, aiming his smoking Colt at the girl.

She instantly closed her mouth. Sobbing, tears rolling out of her dark eyes, she hurled herself off the bed and crawled underneath it.

Claudia looked at her dead lover and then curled a lip at Longarm. "Well, well . . ."

"Where's the . . . ?"

He stopped when he saw the saddlebags hanging over a chair back not six feet from the bed, to Claudia's left. She shuttled her angry gaze from Longarm to the money and then threw herself off the bed, screaming, "*No!*"

Longarm strode over to her just as she drew a pistol up off the seat of the chair. He smacked the gun out of her hand with his left hand, and with more vigor than he'd intended, he smashed the back of his hand holding the Colt across her left cheek.

She flew back against a dresser and dropped to the floor, out like a blown lamp.

Silence.

Longarm lifted his head, listening.

Still, silence. Then Pilar stole quietly into the room, looking around, wide-eyed.

"*Madre de Dios!*" she whispered.

"Yeah, you got that right, girl." Longarm shouldered the bags bulging with the army payroll loot and heaved a deep sigh. He wasn't out of the woods yet, but he sure felt better having the stolen money back in his possession again.

To Pilar, he said, "Do you think you can get us out of here?"

"Us?"

"Yeah," Longarm said, punching the empty shell casings from his Colt's wheel. "You, me, an' "—he looked at the beautiful, naked, comatose Claudia Cordova—"her. Her pa's not far out of town and he'd like a word with her."

Chapter 20

"Yeah, I knew I recognized him!" the man's shout came careening out of the darkness of Longarm's back trail. "That's Custis P. Long, known far and wide as Longarm, all right!"

Longarm and Pilar had managed to slip unnoticed out of the sprawling casa. The two of them had thrown Claudia's dress around the unconscious señorita, and Longarm had draped her across his right shoulder, the saddlebags filled with loot over his left. Now they were halfway down the trail to the dark main street of Poco Carmen, and the thudding of several horses rose behind them, from the direction of Fortuna's outlaw lair.

They must not have gotten away as unnoticed as Longarm had thought. Someone had likely heard the shooting and checked out Fortuna's room to find the outlaw leader dead as last year's Christmas goose. And then Cooper Stanley had put it all together, and now he and several others were closing fast.

Longarm stopped and rasped out to Pilar, "You keep goin'! Head on into town. I'll meet you by that little pink cantina on the corner. That's where my horse is tied!"

"Sí, sí!" Pilar went running off, sandals slapping her heels. Soon her shadow was absorbed by the darkness.

Longarm waited until he could see the silhouettes of the oncoming riders. Then, dropping to a knee, Claudia still draped across his right shoulder, the saddlebags over his left, he raised his Colt and emptied the wheel, the double-action revolver leaping and roaring and stabbing flames back in the direction from which he'd come.

Men and horses screamed. There were the thuds of at least a couple of men falling to the ground. He could hear Stanley bellowing enraged curses.

"Longarm, you son of a bitch!"

The lawman holstered his Colt, rose, and continued running. About a block away from his horse, Claudia stirred and began to struggle.

"Don't give me any trouble, goddammit!" Longarm snapped, seeing Pilar standing in the street lit by a few torches and a distant bonfire. There were four other horses tied with Longarm's brindle bay.

"Longarm," Claudia groaned. "If you take me back to my father, he'll kill me!"

Longarm stopped near Pilar and the horses tied in front of the little pink cantina, the two windows on either side of the propped-open door lit with wan candlelight. He set Claudia down. Bringing a wrist to her cheek, which was swollen where Longarm had smacked her, she staggered back against one of the horses.

"He'll kill me," she sobbed. "He promised . . . the next time . . ."

"Yeah, well, maybe that's what you deserve," Longarm said, throwing the loot-filled saddlebags over the bay's back, behind his saddle. He backed the horse away from the hitchrack and into the street. He looked around for another horse he could confiscate for the purposes of carrying the two women.

"Please," Claudia begged, dropping to her knees before him, tugging on his free hand. "Leave me here, Longarm!" She glanced toward the cantina from which several dark faces stared out of the deep inner murk. Longarm could smell man sweat, mescal, peppery tobacco, and marijuana issuing from the place.

Hooves drummed, growing louder. He looked back in the direction from which he'd come and saw a group of galloping riders swing into the east edge of Poco Carmen.

"Oh, what the hell!" he snarled, and lifted Pilar into his saddle.

"Thank you, Longarm," Claudia said, throwing her hair back behind her shoulders.

Longarm gave the crazy girl a single, fleeting last glance, and then drove heels to the bay's flanks. The horse lunged on up the street, hooves thudding along the twisting trace. Pilar clung to him tightly, arms wrapped around his waist.

He could hear the men from Fortuna's casa behind him. Guns popped. Cooper Stanley shouted epithets.

Just when the pursuers were about to catch up to Longarm and Pilar, bullets screeching through the air around their heads and pluming dust along the night-cloaked trail, the brindle bay crested the hill. Longarm called out to Don Cordova, identifying himself.

The lawman couldn't see the don or any of the don's men—only the wagon in which the Gatling gun bristled like a giant mosquito.

Old Milandro Alvarez crouched behind it, one hand on the crank.

Longarm threw up an arm and shouted, "Cut 'em down, old man!"

He'd barely gotten the last word out before the Gatling gun began rat-a-tat-tatting, belching smoke and fire. In less than a minute, Cooper Stanley and the eight other pursuers lay twisted and dead along the trail.

Peppery powder smoke wafted in the cool desert air.

The old don walked the trail to where Longarm sat the brindle bay with Pilar clinging to him tightly. The don looked at the girl, then at Longarm.

"Claudia?" he asked.

Longarm shook his head. "Sorry, don. She didn't make it."

Longarm couldn't tell for sure, but the old man appeared pleased.

Longarm pinched his hat brim to him, swung the horse around, and trotted on down the hill, heading north toward the border.

Pilar snuggled even tighter against him. She wrapped her arms around the buckle of his cartridge belt. He could feel the warmth of her hands against his belly button. Her small, pointy breasts mashed against his back.

"Oh, thank you, Longarm," the pretty girl sobbed. "Thank you!" She ground her cheek against his back.

"Ah, hell," Longarm said, trying to ignore the warmth spreading throughout his belly and deeper. "No trouble at all."